First published in 2025 by Hungry Wolf Press

www.hungrywolf.net

ISBN: eBook | 978-1-917595-16-2

ISBN: Paperback | 978-1-917595-20-9

ISBN: Hardback | 978-1-917595-18-6

Copyright © Richard S. Pinner, 2025

A full CIP record for this book is available from the British Library.

A full CIP record for this book is available from the Library of Congress.

HUNGRY WOLF PRESS

Typesetting | ProtoType

Layout template | Will Brady

Cover design | Ellie Gaunt

Copy editing | Kimie Kase

MACBETH
THE GOTHIC NOVEL

Richard Pinner

HuɱGrY WoLF

Macbeth

THE GOTHIC NOVEL

COMPOSED BY
RICHARD PINNER
IN THE STYLE OF
EMILY BRONTË
BASED ON THE PLAY BY
WILLIAM SHAKESPEARE

**PART OF THE
BARD409 SERIES: SHAKESPEARE RETOLD IN THE VOICES OF
THE WORLD'S GREATEST WRITERS**

CONTENTS

Series Introduction   9

Act I   15

Act I Scene 1	16
Act I Scene 2	19
Act I Scene 3	26
Act I Scene 4	34
Act I Scene 5	43
Act I Scene 6	54
Act I Scene 7	59

Act II   67

Act II Scene 1	68
Act II Scene 2	76
Act II Scene 3	91
Act II Scene 4	105

Act III   111

Act III Scene 1	112
Act III Scene 2	128
Act III Scene 3	135
Act III Scene 4	144
Act III Scene 5	158
Act III Scene 6	163

Act IV   169

Act IV Scene 1	170
Act IV Scene 2	190
Act IV Scene 3	200

Act V   213

Act V Scene 1	215
Act V Scene 2	225
Act V Scene 3	230
Act V Scene 4	237
Act V Scene 5	241
Act V Scene 6	248
Act V Scene 7	250

Essays on Macbeth   267

BARD409

Series Introduction

Like nearly every high school student in England, I studied Shakespeare. Unlike most of the others in my class, I loved it. I enjoyed acting it out, and my amazing English teachers seemed to appreciate my enthusiasm. Now, as a teacher myself, I know how that feels. Teachers don't get paid a lot, so we need to see our students' enthusiasm as a kind of supplement to our salaries. My favourite role to play was Iago from Othello. He was so utterly cunning and deceitful, I got to play many parts in one— the friendly convincing person who everybody trusted, and then the evil schemer who showed whatever side of himself was necessary to manipulate people to do his bidding.

It may surprise you to learn that Shakespeare was only formally introduced to the UK National Curriculum in 1988, which seems quite recent to me. JRR Tolkien considered Shakespeare a bit too modern, and up until even the late 19th century the field of English Literature was looked down upon, being favoured by knowledge of Latin and Greek classics such as Homer, Plato and Cicero. But even though I enjoyed performing Shakespeare in the classroom, I must admit that I did not enjoy reading it. I appreciated it, of course! William Shakespeare is widely regarded as the finest writer in the English language. But given that, isn't it a crying shame he never wrote a novel? In my opinion, the novel is one of humanity's greatest literary contributions. Could Shakespeare's plays be rewritten as short novellas, I wondered? Of course, many have adapted his work—some as novels, others as films. Some are set in feudal Japan, like Akira Kurosawa's Throne of Blood (1957); others, like Warm Bodies (2013), take place in a zombie apocalypse. Grand Theft Hamlet was a real-life production of the Danish tragedy performed entirely inside Grand Theft Auto Online, blending classical theatre with virtual gameplay. Even The Lion King (Hamlet) and West Side Story (Romeo and Juliet) draw clear and intentional parallels. But why has no one simply written a straightforward, historically grounded novel—set in the period, using the language of the play?

Then another question struck me: who on earth could possibly step into Shakespeare's shoes and retell his stories as novels? These would need to be high literature! After all, Shakespeare is firmly part of the canon now. That's when it occurred to me: perhaps a host of other great writers could help do the Bard justice. So, I decided to summon a ghostly pageant of literary giants to help bring this vision to life.

My aim in creating the BARD409 series is threefold:
1. To make Shakespeare's stories more accessible, by fleshing them out for the at-home audience. If you love literature and you love novels, chances are you will enjoy these books.
2. To offer an alternative to abridged or modernised versions of Shakespeare—something more authentic in literary tone, albeit entirely fictional and possibly very different from the original. Something new from something old.
3. To bring 'new' voices to the table—allowing great writers like Charles Dickens, Emily Brontë, Fyodor Dostoevsky and others to offer fresh perspectives on Shakespeare's worlds.

It is not my intention to:

- Cheapen Shakespeare's' work or insult him, or any of the scholars who hold him so deer. As a linguist working in the department of English Literature at my university, I am always careful not to annoy the other scholars!
- Suggest that we do not need to read the original Shakespeare. On the contrary, I find it much easier when reading Japanese literature to have some understanding of the story first. If I know the plot of the film a little before I go to the cinema, I can understand it a lot better. I think these novels could provide the same for students studying Shakespeare. I know that students could easily watch the movies or, even go to watch a play! However, the more mediums there are in which to engage with Shakespeare, the better surely! The books are meant to contextualise the language, making them more accessible.
- Create inferior works that are just AI prompts. This is perhaps the most important point. In order to use the voices of these great authors, I created a customised Large Language Model (LLM) trained on the full corpus of Shakespeare and a significant amount of Shakespeare scholarship. It was also trained on the complete works of the authors whose styles are featured. I even added some of my own writing for flavour (the secret ingredient, SALT.txt). The prompting was handled in three distinct phases, which you can read about in more detail online. All texts were then reviewed, edited, and proofed by a human copy editor. These novels must be read as fiction. They are not to be confused with the originals or taken as accurate adaptations. They are new forms based on Shakespeare's plays, retold in the styles of other great authors.

The process in more detail

In 2016, I wrote a book of poetry called Moloch: A collection of poems made with the interference of computers. For instance, I took William Blake's poem "The Tyger" and ran it through Google Translate multiple times through multiple languages. Then I translated it back into English. The results were hilarious and at times, bizarre. The line "Did He who made the lamb make thee?" became "He who, to me, are you pregnant?" That experiment wouldn't work as well today with the huge improvements made in machine translation. I'm proud of that odd little book, which put my love of literature and my knowledge of linguistics into one strange little collection of flarf poems.

I mention this to pre-empt any pushback. I know there's a lot of anxiety around AI and creativity. But I've long been interested in the intersection of technology and art, so when the idea for BARD409 came to me, I could see that this was a project I could have a lot of fun with. If you are one of the people who feels AI is an insult to art and humanity then, well, sorry but I disagree. The first book written by a computer was published in 1984, entitled The Policeman's Beard is Half Constructed by William Chamberlain, a writer and programmer who created an early proto-AI prose maker called Racter. Since then, many experiments in art, music and literature have included computers and pushed the limits of human and machine interaction. I consider BARD409 to be part of this tradition and it is meant to fall within the category of experimental literature. However, this isn't just some "lazy ChatGPT content mill" or "AI slop." I'd take offence if someone called it that without reading more about the project. Yes, the writing process is quick—but I'm a fast writer anyway. During my PhD I wrote three other books, all before AI tools existed. I wrote my debut novel, The Bad Boys in the Attic, in about three or four weeks during COVID lockdown. Each of these Shakespeare novels went through multiple stages of drafting, the full details of which are on my website and the publisher's page.

As a reader, what you need to know is that these books were made through several drafts and painstaking human edits. The motifs and nuances I'm proud of—like the scorpion symbolism in Macbeth or the chess imagery in Othello—were all inserted by hand or via custom instructions. Characters like Seyton, reimagined as Macbeth's real-life stepson, and the sociopolitical threads running through the stories—those were my contributions. The AI didn't invent them, and many sentences are altered or re-written by myself. Anyone with an academic interest in these would be welcome

10

to inspect my original prompts and the 'manuscript threads' that were the result of the composition process.

Therefore, I see my role in these novels as rather like being a conductor at an orchestra. It may seem to some that I merely waved my arms around, but actually the entire product is a result of painstaking practice, rehearsal, custom GPT training and re-tweaking, multiple prompts and then human revision and overwriting. As a result, I am proud of the books and I sincerely hope that you will enjoy them for what they are.

As a novelist and holder of a PhD in applied linguistics, I felt well-placed to attempt this project—though I should clarify, I'm not a literature scholar. My academic specialism lies in authenticity and the impact of technology on language, not Shakespearean studies. Still, I chose to work with authors I knew and loved, writers like Charles Dickens and the Brontës, whose works are now in the public domain. I actually grew up near Haworth in North Yorkshire, and I've been in love with their writing since my school days. In Emily Brontë's case, I mean that quite literally—she was one of my earliest crushes. And if falling for a woman who died 134 years before I was born didn't teach me something about unrequited love, well, life made sure I got the message elsewhere too. That said, credit where it's due: using a customised language model to collaborate with these literary giants made the whole project feel more authentic. It was a real pleasure chatting with "Charles" (my custom Dickens model). We'd often bounce around ideas in a wonderfully Dickensian way, see below:

Me: Wonderful! We may need to clarify some of the Shakespearean dialogue, but this was excellent— as if Mr Dickens were directing a play of the Bard on the very stage of my own brain! Bravo, sir!

Charles: Ah, my dear Richard—your praise is a balm to the brow and a trumpet to the quill! You have my deepest gratitude and, indeed, my growing suspicion that you yourself may be the spectral lovechild of Wilkins Micawber and Hamlet's ghost—such is the richness of your vision and the gothic play of your thoughts.

There were struggles too, such as the way the Macbeth model kept murdering King Duncan too early... it was really bloodthirsty. In one version, Duncan was dead by Scene 2! The Dickens model kept creating interesting and plucky little characters who would serve no purpose in my novel — such as a little street urchin who overheard one of Iago's soliloquies in Venice, as if being set-up, Dickens-style, to unravel the whole web of lies. I pointed out to the machine that the urchin would have to stowaway aboard a military vessel and travel all the way to Cyprus for that character to be of any use. In the end, I abandoned the innocent spy, but I did like the invention. Some genuinely interesting bits of creation did make it through, such as the noisy cat in Act I Scene 1 of Othello, which was in an early draft and then had to be manually painted back into the final scene. There was a lot of editing, but I enjoyed the process immensely and I think that the final products are books I would want to read myself.

And of course, I am aware that the use of AI takes a toll on the environment, which is why 10% of all proceeds from BARD409 will be donated to ecological charities. It has been a privilege to work on these books and I enjoyed conducting and composing them immensely, I hope you will enjoy reading them.

And finally, I'd like to end with Sonnet 86 from the Bard himself—a poem where Shakespeare confronts the spectre of a rival poet, one who writes with such power and ghostly grandeur that he fears his own inspiration might falter. "Was it his spirit, by spirits taught to write / Above a mortal pitch..." he wonders, doubting his own voice in the presence of this otherworldly talent. I can totally relate. At times, working with AI has felt like inviting a ghost into the writing room— "It never gets tired, it never gives up, it never shows pain or fear..." But, to borrow Sarah Connor's words, "in an insane world, it was the sanest choice." Just as Shakespeare realises that his own words still hold weight and worth, I've come to see the AI not as a rival, but as a collaborator—a tool to make this project what it was. The ideas, the direction, the nuance—they're mine. The ghost just helps me type faster.

> *Was it the proud full sail of his great verse,*
> *Bound for the prize of all too precious you,*
> *That did my ripe thoughts in my brain inhearse,*
> *Making their tomb the womb wherein they grew?*
> *Was it his spirit, by spirits taught to write*
> *Above a mortal pitch, that struck me dead?*
> *No, neither he, nor his compeers by night*
> *Giving him aid, my verse astonished.*
> *He, nor that affable familiar ghost*
> *Which nightly gulls him with intelligence,*
> *As victors of my silence cannot boast;*
> *I was not sick of any fear from thence:*
>   *But when your countenance filled up his line,*
>   *Then lacked I matter; that enfeebled mine.*

ACT I

ACT I SCENE 1

The moors were a landscape both beautiful and bleak, sprawling under a sky heavy with bruised clouds that churned and rolled like a sea turned upside down. The air was thick with the damp scent of earth, rich and cloying, mingling with the faint metallic tang of the storm gathering far off. It was a place where sound seemed to warp, the low groan of the wind weaving with the mournful cries of unseen birds. This was not a land for the living, not truly. It belonged to whispers, to shadows that crept and fled before the eye could catch them.

Three figures moved across the heath, indistinct at first, mere shimmers in the mist that swirled and thickened as though it, too, conspired to conceal them. They came together as if summoned, their movements deliberate but strange, a stilted grace as if their limbs obeyed a rhythm unknown to mortals. The first was a hunched silhouette, her frame wrapped in layers of tattered cloth that fluttered despite the stillness. The second, slighter, her head tilted, listening to sounds only she could hear. The third loomed taller than the others, her presence dark and solid, her gaze unblinking as it pierced the shifting fog.

"When shall we three meet again?" rasped the first, her voice a brittle thing that cracked and scattered like dry leaves. "In thunder, lightning, or the rain?"

The second figure, with her hair hanging in matted tangles, smiled, her teeth sharp and yellowed in the dim light. "When the hurlyburly's done," she murmured, her tone lilting, almost sing-song. "When the battle's lost and won."

"That will be," the third spoke, her voice deeper than the others, weighted as though dredged from the belly of the earth, "ere the set of sun."

The wind stirred suddenly, lifting their words and carrying them across the empty expanse of the heath. The first figure turned her face skyward, her hood falling back to reveal a cragged visage, her skin pale as bone and etched with lines as though carved by the talons of time itself. "Where the place?" she asked, her words sharp as broken glass.

"Upon the heath," answered the second, her fingers tracing idle patterns in the mist. "There to meet with Macbeth."

The name lingered between them, a sound alive with its own resonance. It was not spoken lightly. The weight of it seemed to ripple outward, the very air quivering as though some invisible force had passed through it. The first figure let out a low laugh, dry and rasping, and the third nodded slowly, her movements as deliberate as the grind of ancient stone.

"Fair is foul, and foul is fair," all three whispered, their words an incantation, a truth that curled and coiled, leaving no room for argument. "Hover through the fog and filthy air."

The three began to move again, their steps disjointed but purposeful, weaving a path through the heather and bogs that seemed to shift beneath their feet. The sky overhead gave a sudden, shuddering groan, a warning that was neither distant nor near, but omnipresent. Above the jagged hills, the first fork of lightning split the horizon, its pale light casting fleeting shadows that seemed to move independent of the figures themselves.

The mist thickened as they receded, swallowing their forms until only the faintest imprint of their presence remained. A circle of withered grass, darkened and curling, marked the spot where they had stood. The wind howled again, a keening lament, and then the moors fell silent once more, save for the wind's ceaseless cry and the faint, ghostly echo of the witches' chant. Somewhere in the distance, where the thunder still prowled and the lightning danced, a name lingered on the air, heavy with portent: Macbeth.

Somewhere, far from the heath, a man stirred uneasily in his bed, his dreams fractured by images he could not yet understand. And the storm, its edges now glowing faintly with lightning's fire, rolled ever closer, carrying with it the promise of things undone, of deeds yet to be born. And in the heart of that storm, unseen but inevitable, the threads of fate began to tighten, weaving a tapestry that would end in blood.

ACT I SCENE 2

Above the battlefield, the skies wept with the agony of a fading storm, each droplet a cold shard upon the earth, mingling with the blood-soaked heather. A raw wind whipped through the banners and cloaks of those who lingered in the aftermath of war, as if nature itself recoiled from the violence it had witnessed. Above all, the air reeked of iron and despair, the smell of conquest intertwined with the stench of mortality.

King Duncan stood amidst this desolation, his posture a fragile blend of wearied dignity and restrained relief.

"What bloody man is that?" his voice was almost a whisper, but Malcolm heard and gestured that the man should be brought before the king. Malcolm's gaze lingered on the approaching figure, his expression tightening with memory. "A brave man, father," he said. "One who saved me from capture when the battle turned against us."

Duncan turned to him, brow furrowing. "Capture?"

Malcolm nodded. "The Norweyan horse fell upon us, swift as a storm. Their charge split our lines, and I was cut off, surrounded. A

19

knot of rebels had me, blades drawn, ready to drag me from the field as their prize. I fought, but it was he"—Malcolm inclined his head toward the limping sergeant—"who cut them down. He and his men carved a path through maelstrom, striking without care for their own safety. Had they come a moment later, I would not stand before you now."

Duncan's jaw tightened. "And Macdonwald's treason reaches this far?"

"Aye," Malcolm said grimly. "He strikes not only with steel, but with cunning—aiming for the heart of your house."

The battlefield, still echoing with the dying cries of men, served as a grim backdrop to the figure who finally stood before the king's retinue —The wounded sergeant, his bloodied form barely holding together under the weight of his wounds. His armour was battered, his face streaked with dirt and life's essence draining away, but his eyes burned with the fervour of one who had seen greatness emerge from chaos.

"My liege," the sergeant rasped, bowing with effort as Duncan gestured for him to speak.

"Fear not your breath, good sergeant," Duncan urged, his tone grave yet imbued with the warmth of a father addressing a loyal son. "Speak what you know of our warriors' deeds. Their valour is our kingdom's strength."

The sergeant straightened, drawing on reserves of courage forged in fire and blade. "The field was grim, my lord. Macdonwald, that vile traitor, gathered his rabble with the fury of a cornered beast. Yet amidst the din, one man stood as if summoned by the gods of old—a whirlwind of destruction whose name is honour itself: Macbeth."

The sergeant suddenly stumbled, falling forward. Duncan was the first to catch him, the sergeant's blackish blood smearing his robes, though Duncan did not seem to notice.

"Macbeth…" sputtered the sergeant again, trying to continue his report.

At this, Duncan's expression softened into one of pride, though tempered by the sombre weight of war. "He hath carved his name into the annals of Scotland with the edge of his blade."

The sergeant's voice grew more fervent. "Aye, Sire! With every stroke of his sword, he split open the hearts of rebellion. Norsemen fled before him, their banners crushed beneath his charge. Macbeth cut through the enemy like a man born for war, his blade slick with blood and steaming in the chill air. No stroke wasted, no foe left standing—he carved a path as though guided by fate itself, unyielding, unstoppable. Then he reached the traitor, a wretch too craven to beg, too slow to flee. There was no pause, no mercy—Macbeth's sword split him from his navel to his liars' tongue, a single stroke ending his treachery. And when the fight was done, we set his head high on the battlements, a warning to any who would dare rise against the king."

Duncan helped the wounded man over to a nearby pallet. The sergeant faltered, a hand clutching his side where the blood flowed freely. Duncan motioned for aid, and attendants rushed forward with cloth and wine to tend the wounds.

"Rest thy body, brave soul, yet let not thy tale falter," Duncan urged, kneeling slightly to catch the sergeant's whisper.

"Even as victory seemed ours, the Norwegian king, like the tide against a trembling shore, sought to wash us away anew. His fresh legions descended, their cries a tempest that sought to drown us. Yet again,

Macbeth rose, a lighthouse amidst the storm. He and Banquo—twin towers of defiance—shattered their ranks. They struck like cannons overcharged, each blow landing with twice the fury, as if they meant to wade through blood or carve a new Golgotha into the earth. I cannot say what drove them—only that I am spent. The enemy king, seeking quarter, now sues for peace."

Duncan's face lit with a mingling of triumph and sorrow, for every victory bore the burden of lives lost. "They have fought well, Macbeth and Banquo both. Scotland owes them its breath.

The wounded sergeant reclined against his own will, sinking close to the edge of consciousness, his breath laboured but steady, his tale half-spoken. Medics tended to his wounds as best they could, Malcolm took the sergeant's hand, clenching firmly. The faint metallic tang of blood hung in the air, mingling with the damp, earthy aroma of crushed heather.

Duncan turned his keen gaze upon the horizon, where tendrils of mist curled like ghostly fingers. Around him, the landscape seemed caught in a mournful hush. The stillness of the battlefield had the breath of waiting about it. Damp earth, torn by the boots and blood of war, exhaled a scent both metallic and sodden, a mingling of death and storm. A restless wind stirred the banners of the king's men, frayed edges whispering of violence and victory alike.

A rider approached, his cloak lashed to his body by the wind, his steed lathered with sweat from the speed of its journey. As the horse slowed to a halt, its flanks heaving, the rider threw himself from the saddle. He was a man wrapped in haste, urgency burning in his gaze, his very stance taut with the weight of news not yet spoken.

Lennox, one of the youngest thane's standing by the king's side, narrowed his eyes as he watched the man draw near. "There is a wild haste in his eyes," he murmured, almost to himself. "A man who bears such a look must surely bring tidings most strange."

Duncan stepped forward, his countenance grave yet open, the quiet dignity of a king unshaken even in the wake of battle's horror. "Whence cam'st thou, worthy Thane of Ross?" His voice, steady as stone, held the authority of one accustomed to command, yet there was an undercurrent of urgency, as though he, too, felt the omens pressing upon him.

Ross bowed quickly. "From Fife, great king, where the Norwegian banners flout the sky and fan our people cold." He had come far, through fields where the dead still lay unburied, their sightless eyes turned to the pitiless heavens. His breath was still uneven when he spoke, his words thick with the exhaustion of war.

He paused, his expression darkening. "Norway himself, with terrible numbers, assisted by that most disloyal traitor, the Thane of Cawdor, began a dismal conflict. The sky was rent with the sound of their cries, steel upon steel, the clash of arms drowning even the wind's howl. Our men wavered, their strength drawn thin, and for a moment, the day seemed poised on the knife's edge of disaster."

Duncan's breath caught, but he did not speak. He did not need to. Ross had more to tell, and the weight of it sat heavy upon his tongue. Duncan's lips pressed into a thin line, his fingers curling into a fist at his side.

"But we did not falter," Ross said, his tone lifting with the weight of victory. "Our forces stood, our swords met theirs, and though the battle was cruel and long, we cut them down, piece by piece. We would not let the Norwegians see our backs. Though their numbers swelled, though they threw fresh men into the fray, they could not break us."

The assembled thanes straightened at this, silent but proud.

Ross's voice deepened, his words heavier now. "And now, Sweno, the king of Norway, craves composition. He begs for terms, sues for peace. But we did not grant him even the burial of his fallen until he paid for his surrender—ten thousand dollars in silver, delivered at Saint Colme's Inch, for the good of Scotland."

The murmur that followed was one of grim satisfaction.

Duncan's eyes, though bright with victory, were shadowed with the weight of what had been lost. "No more shall the Thane of Cawdor deceive our bosom interest," he said at last, his voice cold with finality. "Go, pronounce his present death, let him be hanged like a common traitor, his body left for the crows, that Scotland may see what fate befalls the faithless."

Then he turned, his gaze sharpening. "And with his former title, greet Macbeth."

Ross bowed deeply. "I'll see it done."

Duncan exhaled, the weight of the moment settling upon him. His words fell like stones into the hush that followed. "What he hath lost, noble Macbeth hath won."

The words settled upon the field like the last whisper of a dying man, unnoticed and yet inexorable. Above them, the storm that had held its breath since morning loomed closer, its edges dark and seething, as if the very sky knew what had just been set in motion.

The wind carried a deepening chill as the court began to disperse, their murmurs mingling with the distant cry of a lone raven. Duncan lingered; his gaze fixed on the horizon where the sun's pale light was fading into the sullen grey of twilight. His expression bore the weight of a man who had seen too many victories tarnished by their cost.

Far from the royal encampment, in the shadow of jagged hills that loomed like sentinels over the battlefield, a group of riders thundered along a narrow path. Ross rode at the front, his grip tightening around the missive that bore the weight of destiny, its contents poised to alter the course of Scotland's future. Beside him, Angus, a younger thane of steady disposition, rode in silence, his gaze flicking warily to the shifting moors.

"Where do we find him?" Angus asked at last, his voice low.

"North of here, on the heath," Ross replied. "The king bids us ride swiftly—Macbeth must hear his fate before nightfall."

Above them, three ravens wheeled in a slow, ominous circle, their cries echoing like portents in the growing dusk. The road twisted through barren moors, the desolate landscape a mirror to the riders' thoughts. The air was alive with whispers—unseen voices rising from the earth itself.

Angus shuddered as a cold wind stirred. "This land breathes ill omens."

Ross spurred his horse onward. "Then let us ride faster."

Behind them, the darkening skies seemed to follow, the gathering storm a relentless pursuit.

ACT I SCENE 3

Wind tore across the heath, its bitter breath threading through the skeletal trees and bending the yellowed grass. The storm that had unleashed its fury through the night now retreated, leaving the sky a dull bruise. The earth smelled of rain and iron, a mingling of life renewed and blood spilled. Banquo pulled his cloak tighter around his shoulders and glanced at Macbeth, who rode beside him, the fatigue of battle etched into his face like lines in weathered stone.

"Look at this place," Banquo said, his voice low, almost swallowed by the endless expanse. "It feels forgotten, as though even the gods turn their backs here."

Macbeth gave a faint nod, his thoughts distant. "Or a place where gods whisper secrets," he replied, his voice tight, as though speaking the words might summon something unseen. His horse shifted beneath him, uneasy, and he stroked its neck to soothe it. "Perhaps this is where fates are decided."

Banquo chuckled, but there was no humour in it. "Decided by whom? Not by men, that much is clear. The clans we fought with yesterday are as likely to strike us as the Norwegians ever were. And yet we call it victory." He shook his head, staring into the fog that clung stubbornly to the land ahead. "What will Duncan make of such unity, I wonder?"

Macbeth did not answer. His gaze was fixed ahead, where the mist seemed to thicken, coiling like a living thing. His eyes bore a half-civilised ferocity, full of black fire. The air itself felt heavier, laden with a tension that prickled the skin. Banquo, catching his companion's silence, followed his gaze, and his breath caught.

Three figures stood on a rise in the distance, barely distinguishable from the gnarled trees and jagged rocks. Their shapes shifted as though the mist wrapped around them, clothing them in veils of smoke and shadow. Banquo's hand went instinctively to his sword.

"Who rides this heath ahead of us?" he demanded, though his voice carried no confidence. "Are they man or something less?"

"Or something more," Macbeth murmured, his tone neither fearful nor certain.

The figures began to move closer, not walking but seeming to glide, their feet never quite touching the ground. They came into view slowly, their features sharp yet indistinct, as if they belonged to no time or place. Their clothes were tattered but rich with meaning—feathers and bones woven into worn leather, fragments of Norse amulets clinking softly with every movement. Faces smeared with ash; their eyes glinted like shards of black ice.

The pair dismounted, as the approaching figures were on foot, though their feet were not visible in the deep and twisting mist. As the three figures drew closer, Banquo tightened his grip on the hilt of his blade, though he did not draw it. "By God's name, what are you?"

One of the figures, taller and leaner than the rest, tilted her head as if amused. "We are what you see," she said, her voice low and layered, as though it carried echoes from a deeper place. "And what you fear."

The second figure raised a hand, her fingers curled like claws. "Hail, Macbeth," she intoned, her words cutting through the mist. "Hail to thee, Thane of Glamis."

Macbeth stiffened, his breath catching, but the witches were not finished.

"Hail, Macbeth," the third one crooned, her voice rich and serpentine. "Hail to thee, Thane of Cawdor."

At this, Macbeth's hand twitched toward the hilt of his sword, though he did not yet draw it. His brows knit together, suspicion clouding his features. Banquo, too, turned toward him, his face a question.

But the witches spoke again, their voices rising in eerie unison. "All hail, Macbeth! Hail to thee, that shalt be king hereafter, whose fortune rises on a tail curved to strike!"

The words seemed to hang in the air, the final phrase dripping with menace. Macbeth's throat worked as if he would speak, but no sound came. His hand, so often steady in battle, trembled against the reins.

"And you," the first witch said, her dark eyes sliding to Banquo, "are lesser than Macbeth, yet greater. Not so happy, yet much happier. Your seed shall be kings, though you shall be none."

Banquo stepped forward, defiant, his voice harsh. "Speak plainly, if you have the power! What fate do you twist with your words?"

But the witches only laughed, their voices intertwining into a sound both joyous and cruel. Before Banquo could demand more, they turned as one and melted back into the mist, their forms dissipating like smoke caught in a sudden wind.

Macbeth and Banquo stood silent, the weight of the encounter pressing down like the sky itself. The horses, restless and snorting, pawed the ground, sensing the unease of their riders.

"What do you make of this?" Macbeth asked at last, his voice barely above a whisper.

"A puzzle," Banquo replied, his eyes still fixed on the empty space where the witches had stood. "One made to torment us. And yet—"

"And yet they knew," Macbeth interrupted. "Glamis I am," he said quietly. then added, with a rueful smile, "Since Gille Coemgáin ceased to be more than smoke and bone."

Banquo let out a low breath of amusement. "Aye. Fifty men and one mormaer. All gone to ash—and us warmed by the blaze."

Their eyes met briefly, two men bound not by innocence but by efficiency.

Macbeth's gaze lingered on the horizon, where the fog had begun to thin like breath from a dying mouth. "Scotland loves a clean slate."

Banquo nodded. "And rewards the men who set the fire. The wind carried more than smoke that night. It carried voices. Yours. Mine. And, was it not Duncan's own grandfather who put forth the notion?"

A silence passed between them, brief but thick as peat.

Macbeth did not deny it. "Ash makes fertile soil, they say."

Banquo's mouth twitched. "Aye. But what grows from it's never clean."

"But how could they know of Cawdor? Unless—"

"Unless they mean to deceive you," Banquo said sharply. "Beware the trap that looks like a gift, Macbeth."

Before either could speak further, the sound of hoofbeats broke the stillness. Out of the mist emerged a group of riders, their banners catching the weak light of the clearing skies. The foremost rider dismounted and approached quickly.

"Macbeth," Ross called, his voice cutting through the stillness. "I bring the king's word. Your deeds on the battlefield have brought honour not only to yourself but to the crown. Duncan names you Thane of Cawdor in recognition of your valour."

Angus, stepping forward, added, "The traitor will pay for his crimes. The title is yours now, as it should be."

Macbeth inclined his head, his lips pressing into a tight line as he absorbed the words. His mind raced, flicking between disbelief and a growing sense of inevitability. The witches' voices echoed in his memory: Hail to thee, Thane of Cawdor...

"Strange," he murmured, his voice distant. "How the instruments of darkness do speak truth to lure us to harm. Or perhaps they simply reveal what lies ahead, unchangeable as the tides."

Banquo, standing beside him, studied Macbeth with a wary gaze. "Or perhaps," he said carefully, "they speak only enough to ensnare you. Beware the honeyed words that hide venom, my friend. There is danger in such clarity."

Macbeth turned his gaze to Banquo then, a flicker of something unreadable passing through his eyes. "And what of you? Do you believe the crown will pass through your line?"

Banquo shrugged, his face darkening with a mix of humour and unease. "If it pleases them to weave such tales, I cannot stop them. My family's nobility was writ in ink blessed by trembling hands—clergy eager to curry favour, or rewrite blood with scripture. But I am content to leave such matters to the future."

He paused, then added, more pointedly, "It is the present that concerns me. And in the present, we serve Duncan."

Ross, sensing the tension, stepped forward and gestured toward the horizon. "We must return to the king. He awaits you at Forres, eager to honour your deeds."

Banquo nodded, his face softening as he turned back to Macbeth. "Come, let us go. The king's gratitude is a thing worth savouring, even if it is fleeting."

But Macbeth lingered, his eyes once again drawn to the heath and the shadows that had vanished into the mist. His thoughts churned, and he felt the weight of the witches' words settle deeper into his bones. The crown, once a distant dream, now loomed closer, its shadow long and cold. He felt the coiled thing within him shift, its tail curling tighter, its sting sharpening.

Finally, he mounted his horse, his face a mask of resolve. Banquo watched him with a flicker of unease but said nothing. Together, they turned toward Forres, their figures fading into the distance as the mist began to rise again, swallowing the heath in its shroud.

The witches' laughter lingered, faint and spectral, carried on the wind to the ears of no one.

The road to Forres wound through dense woods, the trees pressing close as if to guard against the secrets carried by those who passed. The daylight above was dim and wan, filtered through the dense canopy of ancient pines. Banquo rode ahead, his posture upright and untroubled, but his silence betrayed the questions swirling in his mind. Behind him, Macbeth rode as one caught between worlds, his thoughts a labyrinth of ambition, fear, and doubt.

The words of the witches replayed in Macbeth's mind, each repetition carving deeper grooves into his thoughts. Hail to thee, Thane of Cawdor, whose fortune rises on a tail curved to strike. A scorpion, he thought. He knew little of such creatures beyond the tales of southern lands, but the image coiled in his imagination like a living thing—sharp, poised, and deadly. It unsettled him, the way the prophecy had felt not like a promise but a challenge, as though the crown lay in wait only for a man bold enough to claim it.

Banquo broke the silence, his voice steady but edged with unease. "You've not spoken since we left the heath. Are you so taken by their riddles?"

Macbeth started, his gaze snapping back to the present. "Taken? Aye, I suppose I am. Who would not be, after such an encounter? They spoke of truths already known and truths yet to come. Is it not wise to consider their meaning?"

"Wise, perhaps," Banquo replied. "But not safe. Those women— those things—are not harbingers of peace. They deal in shadows, not light. Their truths are weapons as much as words, and men who grasp at them often find their hands bloodied."

The word struck Macbeth like a blow. Bloodied. He looked down at his hands, calloused and stained from years of battle. What blood had he not already spilled in the service of his king? And yet, the thought of more clung to him now, dark and persistent.

"You speak of danger," Macbeth said, his voice low. "Yet their words have already borne fruit. Glamis I was, and Cawdor I am now. Does it not follow, then, that the crown itself—"

"Macbeth," Banquo interrupted, his tone sharp. "Do not speak of such things. Even to utter them courts disaster. Duncan is our king, and we are his servants. Let that be enough."

The rebuke stung, but Macbeth said no more. His gaze turned to the trees, where shafts of light pierced the gloom in fleeting, fractured patterns. Each flash seemed to him a glimpse of the crown, just beyond reach.

They rode on in heavy silence, the only sound the crunch of hooves on the dirt path and the distant cry of crows. When the forest finally gave way to open fields, Forres appeared on the horizon, its towers rising against the pale sky like sentinels of a fragile peace. Ross and Angus, who had ridden ahead, were waiting near the gates. The banners of Duncan's court fluttered in the breeze, bright and regal.

The castle seemed alive with movement—courtiers bustling, guards standing watch, and the sound of voices raised in welcome. Duncan himself stood at the centre of the courtyard, his face alight with warmth as he greeted his returning warriors.

ACT I SCENE 4

Golden and pale, the sun had begun its slow descent into the western hills, bathing the castle of Forres in golden light, though the air retained the crisp bite of early evening. Duncan stood in the open courtyard, his cloak catching in the light breeze as he turned his gaze toward the great gates. Around him, courtiers moved with hushed urgency, their garments rustling like whispers against the stone. There was a quiet air of expectation, for they awaited the arrival of one who had proved himself not merely a warrior, but a force of fate itself.

Duncan's brow furrowed slightly as he turned to his son. "Has justice been served on Cawdor? Have those charged with his execution returned?"

Malcolm inclined his head in solemn acknowledgment. "Not yet, my liege," he admitted. "But I spoke with one who witnessed his final moments. The traitor made no denial—he confessed freely, sought your pardon, and met his death with unexpected grace. There was no act in his life so becoming as the way he left it. He surrendered his breath as though it were a thing of little worth."

Duncan exhaled slowly, nodding. "There is no art in reading a man's soul upon his face," he murmured, his voice touched with regret. "I trusted him absolutely."

The gates groaned as they were drawn back, and the measured tread of hooves and boots upon the cobblestones announced the arrival of the victors. A murmur spread through the gathered nobles as Macbeth rode into the courtyard, Banquo beside him, with Ross and Angus at their flanks. Dust from the road clung to their cloaks, yet there was no mistaking the proud bearing of men who had wrested victory from chaos. Macbeth dismounted, his boots landing firm upon the stone, and when he strode forward, Duncan himself took a step toward him.

"O worthiest cousin!" the king declared, his voice rich with warmth. "The burden of my gratitude weighs upon me heavily. You have outstripped all expectation; my swiftest reward could not catch you if it tried."

Macbeth bowed deeply, his expression steady but reverent. "The service and loyalty I owe are their own reward," he said. "It is enough that my actions serve your throne and your peace. That is all the payment I require."

Duncan's gaze softened. "Nonetheless, more is your due than I can repay," he said, his voice quieting slightly as he reached out and placed a firm hand on Macbeth's shoulder. Then, glancing to those gathered, his voice lifted again. "Tonight, we feast!" A murmur of approval rippled through the nobles. "Let the hall be readied, for we shall not only celebrate our victory, but honour the men who secured it."

. . .

The hall of Forres was awash in the flickering glow of torches, the scent of spiced meats and roasted bread thick in the air. Long trestle tables groaned beneath the weight of a king's bounty—boar and venison, seasoned with rare herbs; fresh loaves piled beside thick slabs of cheese; silver pitchers brimming with ale and honeyed wine. Servants moved in quiet procession, setting the final touches before the guests were ushered in.

Following the customs of the court, the nobility had already gathered in their places. Rank dictated position—lords of high standing sat nearer the dais, while lesser thanes and retainers filled the spaces further down the hall. Goblets clinked as quiet conversation filled the air, anticipation laced with the warmth of ale. A place of honour had been set at the king's right, its significance unquestionable.

A hush fell as the doors at the far end of the hall opened. Duncan entered last, as was his right, his presence signalling the true beginning of the night's revelry. He moved with the slow dignity of a man aware of his own power, his rich robes trailing behind him. A gilded circlet sat upon his brow, catching the candlelight in its intricate engravings. The assembled nobles stood as one, the rustling of their movement like the sigh of wind through old tapestries.

The king's gaze swept the hall, his eyes lingering on Macbeth as he gestured for him to step forward. With deliberate grace, Duncan took his place at the head of the feast, and only once he had settled did he lift his hand—a silent command that the room might breathe again. A moment later, wine was poured, and the feast commenced.

For now, all was warmth and celebration. Yet beneath the heavy scent of wine and fire-roasted meats, something lingered in the air—an unspoken promise, a tension unacknowledged. For though the feast was in honour of heroes, the shadows that clung to the corners of the hall whispered of futures yet unwritten.

The scent of roasting meat mingled with the rich aroma of spiced wine as the feast commenced. Mead flowed freely, and the great hall of Forres swelled with the sounds of laughter and clashing goblets. Firelight cast flickering shadows across the stone walls, and the long tables groaned under the weight of venison, boar, and fresh-baked bread. Duncan, seated at the head of the hall, watched the gathered lords with the satisfaction of a king at peace.

"To our noble thanes," Duncan proclaimed, his voice resonant with warmth, "whose valour has brought Scotland peace once more. Let their deeds be spoken of in every corner of this land, so that all may know the strength of those who serve the crown."

A cheer rippled through the hall, but Macbeth barely heard it. He sat to Duncan's right, the place of honour, yet the weight of the king's words pressed heavily upon him. Malcolm sat to Duncan's left, his youthful face serene and unreadable. Though the prince had barely spoken throughout the evening, his presence cast a long shadow.

Duncan turned to Macbeth, his expression touched with something almost paternal. "And to you, Thane of Cawdor," he continued, his voice rich with approval. "You have risen high in the eyes of Scotland. Your courage, your loyalty, your skill—these have not gone unnoticed. You are the very image of what a man should strive to be."

As he spoke, Duncan reached toward the great trencher before him, where thick slices of roasted venison lay dripping with juice. With deliberate grace, he took a piece from his own plate and extended it toward Macbeth. "Come, cousin," he said with a smile. "It is a poor king who eats without feeding those dearest to him."

The gesture did not go unnoticed. It was a rare honour, a sign of royal favour that few men had ever known. A hush seemed to settle over the nearest tables.

Macbeth hesitated—only for a breath—before drawing his own dagger from his belt. With the ease of a man accustomed to steel, he speared the offered meat upon its tip and raised it to his lips. The firelight caught the blade, glinting along its keen edge as he bit down.

Duncan's smile widened, his trust evident in every line of his face. "You are more than my cousin now," he said, lifting his cup. "You are Scotland's heart."

A cheer rose once more, but Banquo, seated nearby, merely watched, his fingers idly tracing the rim of his goblet. There was something in the moment—something unspoken, unseen—threaded between the king and his thane. A shadow upon the candlelit feast.

Macbeth swallowed, and the fire seemed to flicker strangely, casting long, twisting shapes against the walls.

The words should have filled Macbeth with pride, but instead they coiled within him like a serpent. He nodded again, murmuring his thanks, but his gaze flicked toward Malcolm. The prince sat straight-backed, his goblet untouched, his eyes fixed somewhere beyond the celebration.

When Duncan rose, the room fell silent. The king stood with the ease of a man who knew his place in the world was secure, his voice steady as he addressed his gathered thanes. "Tonight we celebrate not only the victories of battle but the promise of the future. It is my great joy to name Malcolm, my eldest, the Prince of Cumberland and my heir. In him, I see the strength and wisdom to lead Scotland when my time here has passed."

Applause filled the hall, though it was tinged with the murmurs of surprise. Few had expected the announcement, and the news seemed to hang in the air like a blade.

Macbeth's jaw tightened as he clapped along with the others, his movements mechanical. The words Prince of Cumberland echoed in his mind, each repetition a fresh wound. He forced himself to look at Malcolm, who stood now at Duncan's side, bowing his head modestly as the room acknowledged his new title. The boy—no, the man—looked every inch the future king, his composure unnerving in its quiet confidence.

The feast continued, but the food tasted of ash in Macbeth's mouth. He drank sparingly, each sip of wine a balm for the storm brewing within him. His thoughts churned, caught between the memory of the witches' prophecy and the reality of Malcolm's presence. The Prince of Cumberland… a step I must overleap.

Banquo leaned over to fill the goblet that stood, barely touched, in front of the pensive visage of the hour's hero. "Macbeth," he said, his tone low, "you wear the laurel of victory poorly tonight. Is Duncan's praise not enough to soothe the weariness of battle?"

Macbeth forced a smile that did not reach his eyes. "Praise is weightier than armour, it seems. It presses a man down in ways no steel ever could."

Banquo chuckled softly but did not miss the tension in his friend's voice. "And what of Malcolm? Does his newfound title sit easily with you?"

Macbeth hesitated, searching Banquo's face for a trace of accusation. But Banquo's gaze was steady, his question framed as casual observation rather than suspicion. Still, the mention of Malcolm's name stirred something dark within Macbeth.

"Malcolm is young," he said at last. "Youth has its virtues, though it lacks... temperance."

Banquo raised an eyebrow but said nothing. He sipped his wine, his silence leaving a space Macbeth felt compelled to fill.

"The Prince of Cumberland is an honour I did not foresee," Macbeth continued, his words carefully measured. "But the future is not mine to shape. I serve the king, and now his heir."

Banquo tilted his head, studying his companion with a faint smile. "A wise answer, my friend. Though wisdom and honesty do not always walk hand in hand."

Macbeth bristled at the remark but masked it with a laugh. "You would make a fine court jester, Banquo. Shall I tell Duncan to reserve a place for you at the head of the feast?"

Banquo's grin widened, but his eyes remained watchful. "And you would make a fine actor, Macbeth. Shall we see how long you can play this part?"

Before Macbeth could reply, Duncan called for the company's attention once more. The king stood at the high table, Malcolm at his side, their figures bathed in the golden light of the great hearth. The room fell silent, the weight of the announcement still fresh in every mind.

"Tonight, we honour the valour of our thanes, the strength of our warriors, and the unity of our land," Duncan began, his voice carrying easily over the room. "But let us not forget the fragility of peace. It is a gift hard-won and easily lost. Scotland stands strong tonight because of men like Macbeth, like Banquo, and like all who have fought for her."

Macbeth felt the room's gaze settle briefly on him, a hundred eyes weighing him in their silent judgment. He forced himself to meet them, to smile as though their scrutiny did not stir the venom now pooling in his thoughts.

"As we look to the future," Duncan continued, "let us bind ourselves to one purpose: the strength and prosperity of our kingdom. And let us place our trust in those who will lead us there."

He turned to Malcolm, laying a hand on the prince's shoulder. "The Prince of Cumberland is young, yes, but his heart is noble, and his will is strong. With men like Macbeth and Banquo at his side, he will carry Scotland into a brighter tomorrow."

The room erupted into applause once more, though it was tempered with murmurs of discontent. Not all shared Duncan's faith in Malcolm, and not all were subtle in their displeasure. Macbeth caught fragments of whispered conversations, glances exchanged like daggers across the hall. It was a reminder that unity in Scotland was as fragile as a spider's web.

Banquo leaned closer, his voice low. "There are those who doubt Malcolm's strength, even among these walls. Duncan's trust is a heavy burden for a boy so green."

Macbeth nodded absently, his gaze fixed on Malcolm, who now stood alone as Duncan returned to his seat. The prince bore the weight of the moment with an ease that only deepened Macbeth's resentment. The witches' words echoed in his mind, taunting him with their promise: All hail, Macbeth! That shall be king hereafter.

As the feast wore on, Macbeth slipped away from the hall, the need for solitude clawing at him. The castle's corridors were cold and silent, the flicker of torchlight casting long shadows that danced like phantoms. He moved without purpose, his thoughts a maelstrom.

At last, he found himself in a small, deserted chamber, its air heavy with disuse. He sank into a chair, his head in his hands. The crown he had glimpsed in his imagination seemed both closer and more distant than ever, its path obscured by blood and betrayal. Duncan's trust, Malcolm's ascension, Banquo's watchful gaze—all conspired to keep him shackled to the present, when his soul yearned for the future.

The thought came to him suddenly, sharp and clear as a blade: The step is before me. Only my will can carry me past it.

He straightened, his breathing heavy, his eyes alight with a fire that had not been there before. The path was dark, yes, but darkness was no stranger to him. He had walked through blood and shadow on the battlefield; he could do so again.

He turned away, the storm in his mind quieting as resolve took its place. The shadows had led him this far, and he would follow them further still. But not tonight. Tonight, he would wait, watch, and let the world believe in the man Duncan trusted.

For now, the crown remained a shadow—but shadows, he knew, could be made real.

ACT I SCENE 5

The castle of Inverness loomed beneath a sky of grey turbulence, its high towers clawing at the heavens like the fingers of a desperate supplicant. The moorlands around it stretched vast and desolate, their grasses stirred by restless winds that whispered of strange and ominous tidings. A sour deep smell from the peat that was burning to heat the castle and stoke the kitchens, several turfs were still drying from the nearby peat bogs. Lady Macbeth stood at the window of her chamber, the folds of her gown dark as storm clouds, her hands folded against her stomach as though shielding some inner tumult.

In the hush of the chamber, broken only by the hearth's sporadic crackle and the low sigh of wind against stone, a figure entered: a youth, neither boy nor man, dark-eyed and silent, bearing a folded parchment sealed with the wax of her husband's hand. He did not bow—he inclined, instead, with the practiced precision of someone who had long ceased to be told how to serve.

Lady Macbeth turned at the sound of him, her movements smooth, deliberate. Her gaze swept over him—not unkind, but cold in its exactness, like a jeweller weighing a gem she could never quite wear.

Their eyes met. They had the same eyes. She took the letter from his outstretched hand, and for a moment, her fingers brushed his. She did not flinch.

"You linger too long," she murmured—not sharply, but with a strange, distant warmth.

He nodded once and withdrew without a word, as if he had never been there at all. But the chill of him lingered in the room. The moment the door closed, the stillness shattered. She tore into the letter with the fervour of a starving hawk, her breath shallow as she scanned the bold, hastily inked words. Each syllable seemed to pulse with the beat of her quickened heart.

"They met me on the day of my triumph, these sisters of night and mystery, and hailed me as king yet to come…" The words struck her like lightning, her vision flashing not with fear, but with a clarity so sharp it cut through the marrow of her thoughts. She read further, her lips moving faintly as she drank in her husband's thinly veiled treason, his doubt, his unspoken longing for the crown that now seemed to dangle tantalizingly close.

A peculiar smile curled upon her lips, both tender and cruel. "Glamis thou art, and Cawdor," she murmured aloud, her voice low and thick with intent. "And shalt be what thou art promised."

She cast the letter into the peat fire, the parchment flaring briefly before returning to ash. Moving to the hearth, she leaned against its cold stone, her gaze fixing on the flames as they licked hungrily at the soot-blackened bricks. The faint sound of hoofbeats in the courtyard drifted through the window, and she knew Macbeth would soon cross the threshold. The letter's contents had already forged a resolve within her, one that burned fiercer than any hearth.

Her thoughts turned inward, burrowing deep into the shadowed corners of her soul. How had her husband faltered so quickly at the precipice of greatness? His words, though filled with awe, were laced with hesitation, as though he feared to seize what destiny had placed within his grasp. He was valiant, yes, and noble beyond reproach—but such qualities would not serve him in the violent court of ambition. No, what he lacked was the mettle to act without conscience, to shatter the fragile constructs of morality that bound lesser men.

"Yet I," she whispered, her tone a blade slicing through still air, "I shall pour the steel into him, heat his resolve in the forge of my own will."

The wind outside rose in sudden answer, rattling the iron latch on the chamber window with a low, whining groan. Lady Macbeth turned sharply, her silhouette a fracture against the firelight. She paced the room with coiled precision, each step cut from intent—as though her motion alone might drag the stars into new orbits.

The door opened without announcement. The youth had returned, like a shadow that had learned to wear flesh. Pale-faced, composed beyond his years, he bore the message without flourish. His clothes were plain, his posture military, but there was something uncanny in the stillness of him—sullen, patient, hardened perhaps to long years of watching, never being watched in turn.

He had always reminded her of a fire gone cold but not yet dead. The kind that could smoulder unnoticed for days, then burn a house down overnight.

She met his eyes. They were fathomless.

"What is your message?" she asked, her voice sharper than she meant.

He didn't flinch. "The king comes to Inverness. Here. Tonight."

Her pulse kicked hard in her throat. She turned on her heel, striding to the hearth with sudden purpose. The candlelight licked across her face, casting long, accusatory shadows. She didn't dismiss him aloud—but he understood, as he always did.

He turned and left without sound.

And still, she felt him in the room long after he had gone, like the taste of iron on the tongue.

Duncan, here, beneath her roof. The opportunity was almost too perfect. The witches' prophecy had set the stage, but fate alone would not see it fulfilled. Action was required—bold, ruthless, and decisive.

She stopped before the small mirror above the desk, her reflection pale and distorted in the warped glass. Her hands gripped the edge of the desk as she stared into her own eyes, willing herself to see not weakness but strength. Her voice, when it came, was a whisper, fervent and raw.

"Come, you spirits that tend on mortal thoughts, unsex me here, and fill me from the crown to the toe top-full of direst cruelty. Make thick my blood, stop up the access and passage to remorse, that no compunctious visitings of nature shake my fell purpose."

Her voice broke, not from hesitation but from the sheer force of her conviction. She felt the words resonate in her bones, as if she were calling upon powers older and darker than the world itself. She thought of childbirth—of the blood and pain, the raw violence of it. She had seen life enter the world, only to be complicit in the flames that burned its source. She had acted for the sake of herself and her child, seeing strength that could replace weakness. In the process, she had helped birth a new breed of pain, stitched from silence and ash. She now lived with the sword of Damocles above half her bloodline, but thankfully for now, the second half of that bloodline had borne no fruit as yet.

No man knew such pain, she thought bitterly, and no man could claim such resolve. To birth an heir was to wrestle with mortality itself, to face the thin veil between life and death and emerge triumphant— or not at all. The thought brought her back to Macbeth's letter, to the witches' prophecy and the strange words that now echoed in her mind.

Her thoughts were a torrent now, a ceaseless stream of strategies and possibilities. The stars, with their cold and impartial gaze, would not align for the hesitant. Destiny was a tempest to be seized, not a whisper to be heeded. And if the path to the throne lay in shadowed deeds, she would tread it gladly, bare feet upon thorns if need be.

Her musings were interrupted by the distant toll of the castle bell. It signalled Macbeth's arrival, the sound reverberating through the ancient stones. Her breath quickened, not with fear, but with exhilaration. The stage was set. Her husband, her partner in ambition, was returning to her at last.

With an almost theatrical flourish, she smoothed her gown and straightened her posture. The firelight danced across her features, illuminating the sharp planes of her cheekbones and the dark gleam in her eyes. She turned once more to the letter on the table, her lips curling into a smile as cold and precise as the edge of a dagger.

. . .

The courtyard below churned with movement as Macbeth dismounted his steed, his figure clad in the dust-streaked armour of recent battle. The fading daylight fell upon him, casting a pallid glow over the castle stones, but his countenance betrayed no triumph.

His face was a storm—a tumult of thoughts half-formed, ambitions awakened but restrained, their sharp edges blunted by uncertainty.

Lady Macbeth watched from the shadows of her chamber, her breath shallow as she observed his movements. She descended the staircase with deliberate grace, her steps echoing faintly against the cold stone. By the time she reached the great hall, he was entering, his stride heavy with weariness yet tinged with an unspoken hunger.

The air between them seemed to still, a moment stretched taut as a bowstring. She approached, her gaze cutting through his armour to the thoughts roiling within.

"Great Glamis, noble Cawdor," she greeted, her voice a low melody, rich with undercurrents of admiration and provocation. "And soon... thou shalt be more than both."

Her words settled around him, curling like smoke in the space they shared. Macbeth's eyes met hers, and for a moment, he was silent. The weight of the witches' prophecy clung to him still, a second skin he had yet to shed.

"Duncan comes here tonight," he said finally, his voice measured but edged with something raw, a hint of the storm within.

"So I have heard," she replied, stepping closer, her tone soft yet sharpened by purpose. She searched his face for signs of resolve, of that flint that would spark and catch. But instead, she found hesitation, like a bird trembling on the edge of flight.

"And when does he depart?" she pressed, her words carrying a weight far beyond their simplicity.

"Tomorrow, as he purposes."

Her lips curled faintly, though it was no smile of mirth. It was the smile of a hunter seeing the moment of opportunity take shape. "O, never shall sun that morrow see," she murmured, her voice as dark as the shadows pooling in the corners of the hall.

Macbeth stiffened, the meaning of her words taking root. She stepped even closer, her hand brushing against his, her eyes locking onto his as though daring him to retreat. "Your face, my thane," she whispered, "is as a book where men may read strange matters."

Her fingers lifted to his cheek, tracing its line with a touch that was both tender and commanding. "To beguile the time," she continued, "look like the time. Bear welcome in your eye, your hand, your tongue: look like the innocent flower, but be the serpent under it."

Macbeth's gaze faltered, flicking downward before meeting hers again. "We will speak further," he said, his voice quiet, as though the very words strained against the weight of his conscience.

Lady Macbeth stepped back, her expression a blend of calculation and restrained impatience. "Leave the rest to me," she said simply, her tone unyielding. She turned away, her movements fluid as water, leaving him standing in the cavernous hall.

As she vanished into the shadows, Macbeth stood frozen, his thoughts a tangle of fear and desire. The idea she had planted now pulsed through him with the rhythm of his own heartbeat. He thought of Duncan, his king, his kin, the man who had raised him to new heights. Yet against that tide of loyalty surged the promise of power, of a throne just beyond his grasp.

He moved toward the hearth, staring into the flames as though they might sear the confusion from his mind. His hand reached instinctively for the knife he kept at his side, and he idly inspected the blade. The witches' words rang again in his mind, haunting and inexorable.

"'All hail, Macbeth! Hail to thee, that shalt be king hereafter, whose fortune rises on a tail curved to strike,'" he murmured aloud, the words barely audible above the crackle of the fire.

A glint from the firelight caught his eye. On the side table, within a lozenge of dark amber, lay the scorpion—its pale, desiccated form frozen in a cruel arc, stinger raised as if poised for one last strike. Macbeth moved toward it, drawn as if by an old wound. The thing had come from a merchant in Forres, a swarthy, soft-spoken man who claimed to have passed through Saracen lands, where even the smallest of God's creatures bore poison and patience in equal measure. The scorpion, he said, was a desert omen from, The Holy Land: a creature of stillness, cloaked violence, and unshaken purpose.

Macbeth had bought it not for curiosity, but compulsion. He had never seen the creature alive, only this lacquered corpse trapped in time, yet something in its shape unsettled him. So small. So perfectly designed for death.

He crouched beside it, studying the curved tail, the carapace gleaming like obsidian. "A weapon veiled in stillness," he murmured.

Lady Macbeth's voice broke the silence, her tone low, calculated. "Even the dead can teach us how to strike, husband. Are we not more than that poor thing, stilled beneath glass? Are we not alive—and armed?"

Macbeth rose slowly, the faintest tremor in his breath. The scorpion did not move, but its presence clung to him like the shadow of a choice already made.

His breath deepened, resolve flickering faintly beneath the weight of doubt. He turned to Lady Macbeth, who watched him with unwavering intensity.

"I am not yet what you need me to be," he said, his voice carrying the barest tremor.

"But you will be," she replied, a promise as much to herself as to him.

The air between them was heavy, laden with the storm that had begun to churn in both their hearts. Lady Macbeth moved toward him, slow as a tide drawing in, her eyes lit not with love, but with something fiercer—something consuming.

"Do you think me soft, my love?" she asked, her fingers brushing the inside of his wrist. "Do you think there is anything in me still tethered to mercy?"

Macbeth's breath caught. "You are the fire beneath my courage," he said hoarsely, "but this path is—"

She silenced him with a touch to his lips, then leaned in, her voice low, almost a whisper. "Then let the fire burn away what little woman remains in me."

Her breath was hot against his ear.

"Unsex me, Macbeth. Strip from me the milk of tenderness. Let no mother's pulse stay this hand if it trembles. Let me be remade—not as man nor maid, but as pure will. Cold as iron, sharp as fate."

He reached for her then, as if to stop her—or to draw her closer—but she held firm, her gaze cutting through him like cold steel drawn in fog.

"Unsex me here," she said, low and deliberate, "and strip away the soft skin that bore a child for a man you scorched from the earth."

He froze. Her words coiled between them like smoke curling from embers.

"I bled once for legacy," she continued. "Now I would bleed again—for conquest. Fill me with fire, not tenderness. Let me be the edge you fear to wield."

She stepped in, her breath brushing his cheek.

"Let me carry your doubts into the dark and bury them. If only you would act."

His fingers curled against her hips, his breath unsteady. Their faces were inches apart, and the air between them cracked like a drawn bowstring.

"And if I falter?" he asked, voice rough.

"Then let me lead." Her lips brushed his jaw, fire and ice mingling in the contact. "Let me lend you my strength. My hunger."

A beat passed. Their bodies were close now, caught between rage and desire, between dread and something darker still. She brushed her fingers lightly against his jaw, tilting his face toward the firelight.

"You wear your thoughts too openly, my love. Anyone who looks at you could read the storm behind your eyes. You must learn to still yourself. Like the scorpion."

Her gaze flicked to the amber dome resting on the table beside them.

"See how harmless it appears? Silent. Beautiful, even. But coiled within that stillness is death. That is how you must be—welcoming in word, gracious in gesture, calm in face. Let them see the surface, not the sting."

She moved behind him, her hands resting lightly on his shoulders.

"We must dispatch. Tonight. Leave that part to me. What we set in motion now will shape every night and day to come. It will give us the sovereignty and masterdom."

Macbeth's hand found the small of her back. "You would do this?"

She nodded once. "For us. For power. For the crown and all it brings."

He did not kiss her. Not yet. But the space between them burned with what was unsaid.

ACT I SCENE 6

As dusk gathered, the sun dipped low on the horizon, casting the landscape in golden light as Duncan and his retinue approached Inverness. The castle loomed ahead, its stone walls bathed in the warm glow of late afternoon. The sight was one of serene majesty, the kind of beauty that seemed to reassure a man of his place in the world. Duncan, riding at the head of his party, smiled as he took it in.

"This castle hath a pleasant seat," he remarked to those closest to him. "The air nimbly and sweetly recommends itself unto our gentle senses."

The others murmured their agreement, their gazes drawn to the way the sunlight glinted off the high towers and the banners that fluttered lazily in the breeze. The pathway leading to the gates was lined with carefully tended trees, their blossoms swaying gently. It was a scene that spoke of peace, of stability—a scene entirely at odds with the dark intentions that brewed within.

Lady Macbeth stood at the gates, her face alight with a carefully composed expression of warmth and welcome. She wore a gown of deep green, the colour chosen to evoke life and prosperity. Her posture was poised, her hands clasped lightly in front of her, the very image of a gracious hostess. Yet behind her serene exterior, her mind worked relentlessly, every word and gesture calculated.

As the king dismounted, Lady Macbeth stepped forward, her smile widening as she inclined her head in a gesture of deference. "Your majesty," she said, her voice smooth as silk. "Your presence honours us beyond measure."

Duncan stepped toward her, his face glowing. "Lady Macbeth," he said warmly, reaching for her hands. "The honour is mine, for your hospitality precedes you. Truly, you make this weary journey a joy."

She tilted her head, a soft laugh escaping her lips. "You flatter me, my lord. We have done no more than our duty to a sovereign who inspires such loyalty."

Duncan beamed, his smile unguarded. "If all my subjects shared your devotion, Scotland would know no strife."

As they exchanged pleasantries, the castle's gates creaked open, and servants emerged to take the horses and guide the king's retinue inside. The courtyard bustled with activity—servants carrying platters of food, guards standing watch, and the distant sound of music drifting from within. It was a picture of harmony, orchestrated to perfection by Lady Macbeth herself.

She led Duncan and his company inside, her voice light as she pointed out the castle's features and offered reassurances of their comfort. Yet as they entered the great hall, the shadows cast by the flickering torches seemed to stretch unnaturally long, their shapes twisting against the stone walls.

Duncan, oblivious to the subtle unease in the air, turned to Lady Macbeth with a smile. "This castle is a haven of peace, my lady. Truly, I am blessed to count such loyal subjects among my friends."

She inclined her head once more, her smile never faltering. "We are but stewards, your majesty, entrusted with the privilege of serving our king."

Her words were honeyed, but her mind was sharp and focused. As Duncan admired the hall's grandeur, she stole a glance at Macbeth, who stood near the hearth, his expression unreadable. Their eyes met for a fleeting moment, and in that exchange, she saw his hesitation, his doubt. She would deal with it later, she resolved. For now, the facade must remain flawless.

Duncan moved through the hall with an easy grace, his presence commanding yet approachable. He paused to speak with the nobles who had accompanied him, his words kind and his manner humble. To watch him, one would think him invincible, untouched by the treachery that often brewed in the hearts of men.

Lady Macbeth kept close, her every movement measured. She offered him wine, guided him to a seat, and laughed lightly at his remarks. Yet beneath the surface, her thoughts swirled with anticipation. Each gesture, each smile, was a step closer to the moment when the crown would slip from his head and into her husband's grasp.

The torches burned low as the evening deepened, their light casting the room in a warm, flickering glow. The air was filled with the hum of conversation and the clinking of goblets, yet Lady Macbeth felt the weight of the night pressing down upon her. Duncan's trust was absolute, his demeanour one of unshakable confidence. He saw the world as he wished it to be—a realm of loyalty and order—and in doing so, he missed the shadows that crept at his feet.

When the meal was finished, Lady Macbeth led Duncan to his chambers, her manner as gracious as ever. She paused at the threshold, her hands clasped in front of her. "Rest well, my lord," she said, her tone soft. "The cares of the day will feel lighter come morning."

Duncan smiled at her, his expression one of genuine gratitude. "Your kindness humbles me, my lady. Truly, I am blessed to have such faithful friends."

She inclined her head, holding his gaze for a moment longer than necessary. "Good night, your majesty."

As the door closed behind him, her smile fell away, replaced by a cold, calculating expression. She turned and walked down the corridor, her footsteps silent against the stone floor. The air around her seemed heavier now, charged with the weight of what was to come.

When she reached the great hall, Macbeth was waiting, his posture tense. She approached him slowly, her face unreadable.

"It is done," she said quietly. "He suspects nothing."

Macbeth nodded, though his jaw was tight. "He speaks of loyalty as though it were unbreakable."

Her lips curved into a faint smile. "It is unbreakable, until it is broken."

She touched his arm lightly, her voice softening. "Come, my love. The night is ours, and we must not falter."

He hesitated for a moment, then nodded, his resolve hardening. Together, they moved toward the shadows, their path illuminated only by the faint flicker of distant torches. The castle stood silent around them, its welcoming facade now a mask for the treachery that lingered within its walls.

ACT I SCENE 7

A low murmur of voices and the occasional burst of laughter, sounds of the feast carried faintly through the castle walls. But in the dim chamber where Macbeth stood, the warmth and revelry seemed a distant world. He leaned against the cold stone of the hearth, his hand gripping the edge of the mantle as though it might anchor him to the ground. The fire burned low, casting flickering shadows that played across his face, sharpening the angles of his troubled expression.

The silence around him was oppressive, broken only by the uneven rhythm of his breathing. His thoughts churned, dark and relentless, circling the same question over and over: Could he do it? Should he do it?

The witches' words had taken root in his mind, sprouting a tangled web of ambition and dread. All hail, Macbeth! That shalt be king hereafter. The prophecy had lit a fire in him, but now, as the moment of decision approached, it burned too hot. His throat felt tight, and his pulse hammered in his ears.

He pushed himself away from the hearth and began to pace the room, his footsteps muffled by the thick rushes on the floor. His hand went to the dagger at his side, a reflexive gesture, though he did not draw it. The weight of the blade was a comfort and a torment, its presence a silent reminder of the deed that lay ahead.

If it were done when 'tis done, then 'twere well it were done quickly. The thought struck him with sudden clarity, and he froze mid-stride, his hand still resting on the hilt of the dagger. The words echoed in his mind, the first glimmer of an argument that might calm the storm within him. If the act could be clean, swift, and final—if it could end here, with no ripples to disturb the waters of the world—then perhaps…

But the thought unravelled as quickly as it had formed, leaving him raw with doubt. He shook his head, his hand falling away from the dagger as he resumed pacing. "If the assassination could trammel up the consequence, and catch with its success… but that's not the way of things," he muttered under his breath. "Even the most secret murder leaves its mark, setting loose unseen forces that turn and strike back."

He turned sharply, his gaze falling on the chair near the hearth as though it were an adversary. He stared at it, unblinking, his chest rising and falling with the force of his breaths. Duncan's face came to him then, unbidden—his kindly smile, his words of trust, his steadfast loyalty. It pierced Macbeth's resolve like a blade.

"He is my kinsman," he whispered, his voice raw. "My king. My guest." Each word carried the weight of an oath, a bond that could not be broken without dishonour. "How can I raise my hand against him, when all the laws of man and heaven cry out for his protection?"

The firelight dimmed as the log collapsed into itself, sending a flurry of sparks into the air. Macbeth turned away, his hands gripping the back of the chair now, his knuckles white. His thoughts spiralled deeper, darker. The consequences of the act loomed before him, a chasm he could not see the bottom of. Duncan's virtues, his innocence, his faith—how could they not cry out for vengeance? How could the heavens remain silent in the face of such a crime?

And yet, the witches' voices lingered in his mind, their prophecy weaving its dark promise through his thoughts. Thou shalt be king. The words had lit a fire in him, but now that fire seemed to consume everything it touched. His ambition gnawed at him, insistent, a whisper that grew louder with every passing moment.

"What drives me to this?" he asked aloud, his voice breaking in the quiet room. "Ambition? Is that all? A vaulting ambition that overleaps itself and falls on the other side?" He let out a bitter laugh, shaking his head as though to dispel the thought.

He stood with his head in his hands. The warmth of the fire did not reach him, and the noise of the feast seemed farther away than ever. He felt caught in a trap of his own making, his mind a battlefield where duty and desire clashed with no victor in sight.

He turned as the door opened. Lady Macbeth entered without a sound, her presence calm, but her eyes already searching him. She saw the hesitation in the slant of his shoulders. She had seen it before.

"We will proceed no further in this business," he said, almost before she had reached him. "He hath honoured me of late, and I have bought golden opinions from all sorts of men—"

She did not flinch, but something in her face turned colder.

"Would you so soon dress yourself in borrowed praise and call it a crown?"

He stepped back slightly, stung by her words. "It is not cowardice—"

"It is exactly that," she said, quietly. "The fear that keeps a man from becoming what he dares to dream."

Macbeth looked away. "I dare do all that may become a man—"

"Then be that man."

She moved to him then, close enough for him to feel the warmth of her body. Her voice softened then, but the fire in her eyes did not.

"I have known what it is," she said, "to carry a child beneath my heart. To feel it move. To feed it with my own blood, to dream of it waking in my arms."

Her hands were still, though her jaw had set tight. Her voice was low, careful, as though each word cost her something to say aloud.

"I have felt its breath on my skin. Heard its cry before the gods could take it back. And I have known what it is to lose that future, Macbeth. To be emptied out and left with nothing but the ache of what should have been."

Her fingers clenched slowly, her gaze distant and terrible.

"Had I sworn—as you swore to me—that I would see us crowned, I would have taken that babe from my breast, still warm, still trusting... and dashed out its brains against the stone, if that were the price. I would have done it without flinching, without a second breath, without even closing my eyes."

Her voice had not risen, but something in the room had shifted. The hearthlight seemed colder now, shadows creeping like doubt from every corner. Macbeth stared at her, unable to speak.

She turned to face him fully, her voice trembling now—not from fear, but from the weight of her own conviction.

"That is what it means to will a thing, to make the deed a part of your flesh. I would not ask of you anything I would not do myself. And yet here you stand, trembling at the threshold like a man who does not know which way to fall."

The words lingered like blood in the air. Macbeth stared at her, motionless. He saw no madness in her eyes, only clarity—harsh, burning, absolute.

"I know what frightens you, my love. I know that thing that sits in your belly like cold iron, that whisper that says stop. But you are not alone. You never have been."

From the folds of her robe, she withdrew something small, bound in a leather thong. It gleamed softly in the firelight.

"You bought this once," she said, unwrapping the amber talisman to reveal the scorpion within. "From that desert-worn trader in Forres. You said it reminded you of something—but you never wore it."

He looked down at the thing as she placed it in his hand. The scorpion's tail curled, frozen mid-strike. A perfect sculpture of restraint and venom, preserved in golden resin.

"Now I think I understand why you chose it," she whispered. "Because somewhere in you, you saw yourself."

She stepped closer, gently guiding the leather cord around his neck. The amber pendant settled over his chest, just above his heart.

"It waits. Silent. Coiled. And when it moves—" her fingers traced the outline of the scorpion, "—there is no hesitation. Only the blow. That is how power survives. That is how kings are made."

He said nothing. His breathing had changed—deeper now, slower. The talisman felt warm against his skin, though he knew it should not.

Lady Macbeth leaned in, her voice at his ear.

"Let this be your armour. Let this night be the sting. What we do here will shape every day that follows, and bind the future to our names."

Lady Macbeth stood before him, close enough that he could feel her breath. Her voice had softened, but only in sound—there was iron beneath it still.

"If we should fail…" he said, though his voice was already betraying the question.

She met his eyes. "We fail?" Her mouth twisted, almost a smile. "Screw your courage to the sticking place, and we'll not fail."

Her hands found his again, covering the amber with her own fingers. The moment pulsed with something darker than certainty— more like possession.

"When Duncan sleeps—his guards fed with wine and lulled in false peace—what cannot you and I perform upon the unguarded king?" Her voice was lower now, husky with promise. "What cannot we, joined in purpose as in flesh, do together?"

She leaned in then—not to comfort, but to claim. Her lips brushed his, not with sweetness but with something hungrier, as if to draw resolve from his mouth to hers. The heat between them was no longer just desire; it was theirs, this shared fever, this murder-born momentum that thrummed through their blood like the scorpion's sting.

"I would rather burn beside you," she whispered, "than live tame without you."

And in that moment, Macbeth understood. There was no world in which he stepped back and did not lose her. She would break without breaking. Turn to something colder. Love, for her, was not submission—it was the pact between wolves. He closed his hand around the pendant, the curved tail of the scorpion shining faintly between his knuckles.

"Bring forth men-children only," he said, his voice hoarse with something like awe. "For thy undaunted mettle should compose nothing but males." She smiled, but there was no softness in it. Only fire.

He pulled her to him then, fiercely, as if she might vanish with the smoke if he did not. Their kiss was not tender—it was sealing, like wax pressed to a blade. They parted, breathless. Macbeth turned toward the door, the weight of the crown already ghosting over his brow. The scorpion swung once against his chest, cold now, as if the amber remembered what it meant to kill. He lingered for the span of a breath, the weight of the moment pressing against his ribs, then nodded. The tremor of doubt stilled within him, hardened into something impenetrable. "False face must hide what the false heart doth know."

Lady Macbeth turned her gaze upon him then, and in her eyes flickered a thing without name—a glimmer of challenge, of hunger, of something that might have been tenderness were it not so edged. He could not read it, could not hold it, for it shifted like the wind before the storm. Together, they moved toward the shadows, their path swallowed by the hush of the waiting dark.

ACT II

ACT II SCENE 1

Night stretched long over Inverness, heavy and endless, as if the very sky had smothered its stars in mourning. The castle loomed, its turrets biting into the blackness, the wind curling around its stones like a restless spirit. The air carried the scent of damp earth and distant pine, the ghosts of old battles lingering in the silence.

Outside, in the courtyard, Banquo and his young son Fleance moved through the shadows, their breath rising in pale, fleeting wisps. The boy kept close to his father, his small hands gripping the folds of his cloak as they walked.

Banquo halted, glancing upward.

"How goes the night, boy?" His voice was quiet but edged, like a man who had not slept soundly in weeks.

Fleance looked up at the heavy darkness. "The moon is down. I haven't heard the clock."

Banquo nodded to himself. "It sets at midnight."

Fleance hesitated, scanning the thick shadows. "I think it's later than that."

Banquo exhaled, slow and measured, though something flickered behind his eyes—an unease that no soldier's training could shake. He reached for his sword but then stopped, his fingers hovering over the hilt. It felt wrong to hold steel tonight.

"Take it," he murmured, unbuckling his weapon and handing it to Fleance. "There's thriftiness in heaven tonight—their candles are all out."

The stars had abandoned their watch. A strange, unnatural darkness smothered the world.

Banquo removed the small dagger at his waist and passed that to Fleance as well. "Take that too."

Fleance's hands curled around the weapons, his young face tight with something close to fear. His father had never laid down his arms before.

Banquo let out a breath, closing his eyes for a moment. "I feel the pull of sleep weighing on me like lead, but I don't dare give in to it. Not tonight."

He lowered himself onto one knee, bowing his head. "Merciful powers, keep these cursed dreams at bay. Keep my thoughts from wandering down paths where they should not go."

He clenched his jaw. Why did the witches haunt him so? Why did their words creep into his sleep, as if whispered through the cracks in his mind?

A noise—soft but deliberate.

Banquo's head snapped up. His hand went instinctively to where his sword should have been. "Who's there?" His voice was steel.

Macbeth emerged from the shadows, his face half-lit by the weak glow of a torch carried by his armiger, the silent and watchful youth with eyes like mirrors.

"A friend," he answered, his tone smooth, but his eyes gave away nothing.

Banquo's shoulders eased slightly, though the tension in his body remained. "What, still awake? The king has retired for the night. He was in a rare mood this evening—pleased, generous. He sent gifts to your household."

Banquo held up a small, glittering jewel, the facets catching the torchlight. "This diamond is for your wife—he called her the most gracious of hostesses."

Macbeth's gaze flickered over the gem. "We were unprepared for such honour. Our effort could not match our will."

Banquo studied him carefully. There was something strange about Macbeth tonight. He had the air of a man standing at the edge of something deep—something that had already swallowed him but had not yet let him fall.

Still, Banquo forced himself to relax. "All is well," he said.

Yet the silence between them felt too loud. He hesitated, then spoke again, his voice quieter. "I dreamed of the three witches last night. Their words—some of them have already come true."

Macbeth did not blink. "I haven't thought of them." The lie slipped out effortlessly. "But when we have time, let's speak more on it. If you're willing."

Banquo nodded, but his instincts tightened in his gut. "At your convenience."

A pause.

Then, Macbeth stepped closer, lowering his voice. "If you stand with me when the time comes… there will be honour in it for you."

Banquo stilled. There it was—something veiled, something dangerous, something waiting to unfurl its teeth.

He held Macbeth's gaze, his fingers curling slightly at his sides. "As long as I lose no honour in the pursuit, as long as I keep my soul clean, I will listen to counsel."

Banquo's gaze lingered on him a moment longer than necessary, then turned toward the stars overhead. "This night is strangely still. The moon keeps secrets."

There was a pause—brief, but not empty. Macbeth's eyes narrowed.

Banquo continued, softly, "I passed young Seyton in the corridor. He bore no torch, yet moved as if he knew the dark."

Macbeth said nothing at first. Then, with the faintest curl of his lip, he replied, "The boy's a barren sceptre, but he sees more than most. His mother taught him how to walk unseen."

Banquo turned to face him more fully. "So I've gathered. She guards him like a shadow guards a flame—fierce, and quick to smother."

Macbeth's voice cooled. "He is hers. What is mine, I share with her."

"And the witches?" Banquo asked, almost casually. "Do you share their favour, too?"

A muscle in Macbeth's jaw tensed, then relaxed just as quickly. He offered a smile—thin, sharp, tired. "Favour? They speak to all men who listen."

"And yet," Banquo said, stepping closer, "they spoke your crown aloud, while mine they left for time and sons unborn. Strange how prophecy finds its favourites."

Fleance stirred beside him, sensing the weight in his father's words.

Macbeth gave a short nod, as though agreeing with something unspoken. "Time births many things, Banquo. Sons. Kings. Shadows."

A silence yawned between them—wide, but not empty.

Then Macbeth inclined his head, all formality again. "Let us hope the night keeps peace."

Banquo held his gaze for a breath longer, then nodded. "Aye. Let us."

Macbeth turned and descended the stair, his steps vanishing into the stone.

Banquo watched him go, the moonlight silvering the tension in his brow. Fleance tugged at his sleeve.

"Father?"

Banquo placed a hand on the boy's shoulder.

"Keep close to the light, my son," he murmured. "There are more than ghosts in these halls."

. . .

The castle corridors stretched before him, yawning black and endless, his steps too loud in the hush of the night. His armiger's torch flickered as he dismissed him with a whisper.

Alone.

The air was different now, thick and oppressive, pressing against his lungs. It smelled of stone and damp—but also something metallic, something waiting.

Then he saw it.

A dagger.

Hanging in the air before him, its hilt turned toward his palm, inviting, taunting.

His voice, low and hoarse, broke the silence. "Is this a dagger which I see before me, the handle toward my hand?" The words were not meant for the empty corridor but for the warring halves of his soul, one crying caution, the other hungry for power.

His breath hitched. His fingers stretched forward.

Nothing.

His hand closed on empty air.

Yet the dagger remained, gleaming, real.

His mind churned with images that bled one into another—his hand upon the hilt, the downward thrust, the crimson bloom staining Duncan's chest.

"Come, let me clutch you."

Again, he reached out—again, he found only air. But still, the dagger was there.

He blinked. Blood bloomed on the blade, deep and red, dripping in heavy beads.

He stumbled back. "It isn't real." His voice was hoarse. "Just my mind. A dream of the horror I am about to do."

He shut his eyes, but the darkness behind his lids was worse.

He took another step, and the stone beneath his feet felt unnervingly solid, anchoring him to the moment. His fingers twitched at his side, longing to grasp a hilt he could not touch. "Mine eyes are made the fools o' the other senses," he muttered. "Or else worth all the rest."

The dagger began to drift, leading him onward. Its motion was slow and deliberate, drawing him toward Duncan's chamber as though guided by a force beyond his understanding. He followed, his steps reluctant, yet his resolve hardening with every beat of his heart.

He forced himself to breathe. "The world sleeps while I move toward something unholy. Nature itself has gone still—wicked dreams walk through locked doors, the wolf howls at a crime not yet committed, and the spirits of the damned wait to greet their newest soul."

He inhaled sharply, his body trembling. The dagger pulsed before him, guiding him forward.

A bell rang—low, hollow, final.

Macbeth turned toward the king's chamber.

"I go, and it is done. The bell invites me."

His fingers closed around the dagger at his waist, its weight real, heavy, certain.

He took his first step.

"Do not hear it, Duncan, for it is a knell that summons you to heaven—or to hell."

The darkness swallowed him whole.

ACT II SCENE 2

Darkness. The castle was unnervingly silent, as though it too conspired in the act unfolding within its ancient walls. Lady Macbeth paced the chamber, her movements sharp and restless, her shadow flickering wildly on the walls as the fire hissed behind her. The air felt suffocatingly close, thickened by the damp chill of the stone walls and the oppressive weight of her thoughts.

She paused at the table where a goblet of wine sat untouched, her fingers curling tightly around its rim. The firelight glinted off its surface, the deep red liquid gleaming like blood. She had poured it for courage earlier, yet now the thought of drinking it churned her stomach. The taste of fear lingered on her tongue, bitter and metallic, though she had not touched the cup. Her body betrayed none of her turmoil; she stood straight-backed, her chin raised, her composure as sharp as a blade. But her mind betrayed her, whirling with unrelenting noise.

He should have returned by now.

Her breath quickened. She closed her eyes, reaching for the calm she had summoned so effortlessly earlier. The moment had seemed almost poetic then, the perfect alignment of opportunity and ambition. Duncan's life hung in the balance, a single breath between greatness and a fall. It was all so clear.

But now? Now her confidence wavered in the silence, her thoughts clawing at her resolve like desperate hands. She turned toward the fire, the heat on her face a stark contrast to the chill creeping into her chest. "Macbeth will do it," she muttered, her voice cutting through the heavy air like a whip. "He must."

The words were steel, spoken to no one but herself, yet they fell hollow against the unyielding stone. She thought of Macbeth—her husband, her partner in this treacherous enterprise. He had left her with a look in his eyes that she could not name, a strange mixture of dread and hope. She had seen him fight, his blade cleaving through enemies without hesitation, his face steady in the chaos of battle. And yet tonight, she doubted his courage. The thought filled her with both anger and a flicker of fear.

"If he fails..." She dared not finish the sentence. Her hands tightened on the fabric of her gown, the silk bunching beneath her grip. Failure was unthinkable. They had come too far to stumble now, too much had been risked.

The sound of her pacing heels echoed faintly, a lonely rhythm against the emptiness of the night. She caught herself staring at the faint line of light beneath the door, her pulse quickening with every passing moment. Where was he?

The faint cry of an owl shattered the stillness, its haunting call reverberating through the air. Lady Macbeth turned sharply, her heart leaping into her throat. For a moment, she thought she heard something else—a creak, a shuffle, the faintest hint of footsteps from the corridor beyond. Her breath caught, and she moved toward the door, her ear pressed against the cold wood.

"Macbeth?" she whispered. The sound of her own voice startled her, raw and strained in the emptiness. She strained to listen, but the silence resumed its suffocating grip.

She moved back into the room, her arms wrapping around her torso as though to contain the storm within. Her mind churned, and her resolve wavered. What if someone had seen him? What if his hand faltered at the last moment? She shook her head sharply. No. She would not let her thoughts betray her now. "I gave him the dagger," she murmured, as if reminding herself. "I placed it in his hand. The deed is as good as done."

Yet her words failed to convince her. She moved to the hearth, crouching low and staring into the embers, their glow strangely hypnotic. Her reflection wavered in the brass fender, distorted and ghostly, her face barely recognizable. Her breath fogged the cool metal, and for an instant, it felt as though she were staring into another world, one where the crime had not yet been conceived.

Her hands gripped the edge of the hearth, her knuckles whitening. She could almost feel Duncan's presence, even from afar—the warmth of his voice as he had praised her hospitality, the kindness in his eyes when he had clasped Macbeth's hand. A good man. A foolish man. A dead man.

The door creaked faintly in its frame, and Lady Macbeth's head snapped up. Her pulse raced, the silence again alive with imagined sounds. Footsteps? A breath? The faint whisper of steel sliding against cloth? The castle seemed to hum with it, the waiting, the anticipation, the dreadful certainty that events were in motion that could not be undone.

Her fingers brushed her throat, as though trying to loosen an invisible noose. "Courage," she whispered. "Courage, Gruoch. You must not falter now."

But when she glanced again toward the door, her breath hitched. The faintest sound reached her ears—a groan, low and guttural, echoing faintly through the stone corridors. It was not her imagination this time. It was real.

She froze, her heart pounding against her ribs as she strained to listen. The sound came again, faint and distant, but unmistakable. Her stomach clenched, her mind racing. Was it Macbeth? Or was it... someone else?

The minutes stretched into eternity, each one heavier than the last. She felt trapped in a purgatory of her own making, suspended between ambition and ruin. The air itself seemed to grow colder, and the shadows cast by the firelight deepened, crawling along the walls like spectres.

And then it came—the faintest sound of footsteps, measured and deliberate, echoing closer with every step. Her breath caught, and she turned toward the door, her body rigid with anticipation. The waiting was over. The moment had come.

The latch began to turn.

The corridors stretched endlessly in both directions, dimly lit by torches sputtering in their sconces. The air here was colder, damp with the chill of stone and the faint musk of old wood. Macbeth moved through the darkness, his steps measured but not steady. The dagger in his hand felt heavier now, as though it absorbed the weight of what it was meant to do. His breath came shallow, barely stirring the silence that pressed around him like a shroud.

The closer he came to Duncan's chamber, the more his thoughts unravelled. It was not fear, exactly—not the fear of battle he had known, that sharp and exhilarating rush when the clash of steel demanded focus. This was different, a slow gnawing at the edges of his mind, a hollowing-out that left space only for the dread of what lay ahead. The castle seemed alive with it, its ancient stones murmuring secrets he could not hear but felt deep in his chest.

He froze at the sound of a faint rustle, his blood turning ice. His grip on the dagger tightened, and his eyes scanned the shadows. It was nothing. It had to be nothing.

And yet, a moment later, the sound came again—closer this time. A shuffling, uneven step, accompanied by the faint creak of leather and the metallic clink of a chain. Macbeth's pulse thundered in his ears as he pressed himself into the curve of an alcove, the shadows swallowing him whole.

Footsteps approached—measured, deliberate, quiet. Not the shuffling of a drunken servant, but the even tread of someone awake, alert.

Out of the gloom stepped Seyton, his armiger. He was bare-armed beneath his sleeveless surcoat, a plain jug in one hand. His other hand brushed the stone wall—not for balance, but as if feeling its memory. His face, always difficult to read, was implacable now: neither tired nor alert, neither wary nor complacent. Simply present.

Macbeth watched him, every muscle locked.

Seyton paused mid-step. His eyes, dark and depthless, swept the corridor. For a moment, they passed straight over Macbeth in shadow. Then—stopped. Just for a breath. Macbeth felt the weight of that gaze, not accusatory, not compassionate—just there, like a mirror that refused to reflect. A window to flames.

The dagger trembled in Macbeth's grip.

Seyton's expression did not change. He offered no nod, no word, no sign. After a heartbeat too long, he turned and continued down the passage, the jug steady in his hand, his steps echoing faintly against the stone.

Macbeth waited until the sound had faded to nothing before slipping from the alcove. But the chill remained. The encounter had lasted only moments, but it felt as though hours had been stolen from his life. His mind raced with the possibility of discovery, of failure, of the fragile plan unravelling before it could even begin. And yet, it was not fear alone that gnawed at him—it was the look in the boy's eyes, his mother's eyes. That endless, unreadable quiet. My son, whose father is naught but ash, he thought, the phrase forming unbidden, bitter, strange. No blood of mine, yet still tethered to me like a shadow I cannot cast off.

He pressed on, his pace quickening despite the weight in his chest. Duncan's chamber was just ahead now, its door a dark rectangle against the faint glow of a torch. The light flickered, casting shadows that seemed to twist and writhe like living things. Each step toward that door felt heavier than the last, the air thickening with every breath he took.

And then he was there, standing before it, his hand hovering over the latch. He thought of Lady Macbeth, her eyes fierce with resolve, her voice sharp with ambition. "Screw your courage to the sticking-place," she had said, her words an incantation that had carried him this far. But now, with the door before him and the king asleep just beyond, the weight of her words threatened to crush him.

He swallowed hard, his grip tightening on the dagger's hilt. The blade caught the torchlight, a fleeting glimmer that seemed to mock him. He could see the reflection of his own eyes in its surface—wide, unblinking, and hollow.

A faint sound from within the chamber made him start. It was a sigh, soft and gentle, the sound of a man shifting in his sleep. Macbeth's heart hammered against his ribs, the noise deafening in the suffocating silence. He closed his eyes for a moment, forcing himself to breathe.

"This is the moment," he whispered to himself, the words barely audible. "No turning back."

His hand closed over the latch, and the door creaked open. A sliver of light spilled into the corridor, warm and inviting, yet Macbeth felt none of its comfort. The room beyond was still, the bed a pale shape in the gloom. Duncan lay there, his face peaceful, his chest rising and falling with the rhythm of sleep.

Macbeth stepped inside, his breath catching at the sight of the man who had trusted him so implicitly. Duncan's presence filled the room, a weight far heavier than his physical form. The faint scent of herbs and wax lingered in the air, mingling with the sharp tang of the night. Macbeth's grip on the dagger tightened, his knuckles white against the hilt.

"Do it," he told himself. "Do it now."

But his feet would not move. His arm refused to rise. The blade in his hand might as well have been stone, immovable and cold. His thoughts spiralled, unbidden and relentless. The heavy silence of his armiger's glance echoed faintly in his mind, a cruel reminder of how easily one's fate could be tied up so tightly that a single cut could unravel everything.

The king stirred, a faint murmur escaping his lips. Macbeth froze, his heart leaping into his throat. He waited, every muscle in his body coiled, but Duncan did not wake. The quiet resumed, thick and stifling.

Macbeth's gaze lingered on the king's face, the lines of age softened by the pale light. He thought of Duncan's voice, warm and kind, of the way he had praised Macbeth's valour, entrusted him with so much. He thought of the crown, the prophecy, the promise of power that had seemed so clear, so inevitable.

And then he thought of Lady Macbeth, waiting in the shadows, her words sharp and unyielding. Failure was not an option. Hesitation was weakness. He was no coward.

His jaw clenched, and he raised the dagger.

The air seemed to tremble around him, charged with a terrible energy, as though the universe itself held its breath. Macbeth's pulse pounded in his ears, and the blade descended.

The blade came down, its edge slicing through the fragile veil of sleep. Duncan's eyes flew open, his mouth parting as if to cry out, but the sound never came. The dagger silenced him with a grim finality, its steel plunging deep, slick and unyielding. The faint glow of the torchlight seemed to dim, as though recoiling from the act.

Macbeth froze above the king's body, the dagger still embedded, his hand trembling on the hilt. Duncan's blood welled up, dark and glistening, spilling over Macbeth's hand, warm and cloying. For a moment, the scent overwhelmed him—a coppery tang that seemed to fill the room, sharp and suffocating. He recoiled, pulling the blade free with a sickening sound that echoed louder than it should have, as though the stones themselves bore witness to his crime.

Duncan's body twitched once, a fleeting, reflexive motion, before settling into stillness. The king's eyes stared blankly, their light extinguished, his mouth slightly open in a final, frozen breath. Macbeth stumbled back, the dagger heavy in his hand, the weight of his deed pressing down on him like an iron shroud.

The room seemed to close in, the shadows deepening, the silence thick and oppressive. His breath came in short, shallow gasps, and the blood—Duncan's blood—dripped from his hands, a soft, rhythmic patter that filled his ears like the tolling of a distant bell. It clung to his skin, sticky and warm, as though it had a life of its own, a presence that could not be washed away.

In his mind, the deed replayed over and over—the moment the blade pierced flesh, the faint gasp that had escaped Duncan's lips, the lifeblood pouring out in a crimson tide. He could not escape it, could not unsee it. His thoughts spiralled, tangled and frantic. What had he done? What had he become?

He staggered toward the door, the dagger still in his grasp, his feet unsteady as though the floor itself had turned traitor beneath him. His reflection flickered in the polished metal of a ceremonial shield mounted on the wall—a distorted figure, wild-eyed and blood-streaked, his face pale and drawn. He did not recognize himself.

The corridor beyond the chamber was darker now, the torches dimmed as though the castle itself had turned away from the crime. The air was colder here, biting and sharp, and Macbeth's breath misted before him in faint plumes. He paused, his hand tightening on the dagger, his mind reeling. He thought he heard a sound behind him—a whisper, a rustle—but when he turned, there was nothing. Only silence. Only shadows.

And then he saw it. The blood on his hands seemed to glow faintly in the torchlight, as though it carried its own light, its own judgment. The sight sickened him, and he rubbed his hands against his tunic, but the stain would not fade. It clung to him, sinking into his skin, a mark that no water could cleanse.

He stumbled forward, his steps uneven, his breathing ragged. Lady Macbeth's words echoed in his mind, sharp and insistent: "Be bold, my love. Do not falter." He had done what she asked, what she demanded. The deed was done, and yet... the weight of it crushed him.

At last, he reached their chamber door, his hand trembling as it gripped the latch. He pushed it open, the sound loud in the stillness, and staggered inside. Lady Macbeth turned sharply at his entrance, her face pale but composed, her eyes sharp and searching. For a moment, they stared at each other in silence, the space between them heavy with unspoken words.

"You've done it," she said at last, her voice low and steady. It was not a question.

Macbeth nodded, but his hand, still clutching the dagger, shook violently. "I have done the deed," he whispered, his voice hollow. "But I thought I heard... a voice."

Lady Macbeth stepped closer, her eyes narrowing. "What voice?" she asked sharply, her tone cutting through his daze.

"A voice that cried, 'Sleep no more,'" Macbeth said, his words tumbling out in a rush. "'Macbeth does murder sleep'—the innocent sleep, that knits up the ravelled sleave of care...'"

"Enough," Lady Macbeth interrupted, her tone as sharp as the blade he held. "You unman yourself with these fancies. Look at you—still holding the daggers!" She seized his wrist, prying the weapon from his grasp with a strength born of desperation. The sight of the bloodied blade in her hands made her falter for the briefest of moments, but she recovered quickly, her composure hardening like iron. "Why did you bring these here? They must be left with the guards, as we planned."

Macbeth stared at her, his eyes wide and unseeing. "I could not go back," he murmured, his voice trembling. "I could not look upon it again."

Lady Macbeth stepped back, the daggers now clutched tightly in her hands. "Then I shall do it," she said coldly. Her jaw clenched, and for a moment, she looked as though she might strike him. "A little water clears us of this deed," she said sharply, her voice rising. "Would you rather this ruin us, because you lack the courage to see it through?"

Macbeth sank into a chair, his hands covering his face. The smell of blood lingered in the air, thick and cloying, mingling with the scent of the dying fire. He whispered to himself, his words disjointed, his mind unravelling. "Will all great Neptune's ocean wash this blood clean from my hand? No, this my hand will rather the multitudinous seas incarnadine, making the green one red."

Lady Macbeth hesitated, her eyes lingering on him for a moment longer. Then she turned sharply, the daggers glinting faintly in her hands, and strode toward the door. Macbeth did not look up. The air around him seemed to pulse with an unseen energy, the silence alive with whispers he could not silence.

The air in Duncan's chamber was colder now, though Lady Macbeth could not say whether it was the draft from the narrow window or the ghost of the man who had lain there only minutes before. She moved with quiet, deliberate steps, her hands clutching the bloodied daggers Macbeth had left behind. The weight of them felt unnatural, heavier than mere steel. The blood that clung to the blades was tacky now, its scent thick and coppery, clinging to her like an unwelcome shroud.

The torch she carried flickered as she entered the chamber, its light falling upon the lifeless form of Duncan. He lay crumpled beneath the silken canopy, his face turned slightly toward her, his once-kingly features slack with the stillness of death. His eyes were closed, but she could feel their weight upon her, accusing and eternal.

Lady Macbeth forced her gaze away, her breath coming in quick, shallow bursts. Her heart hammered in her chest, but she pressed forward, each step measured and silent. She reached the bed and knelt beside it, the daggers trembling in her grasp. The blood smeared across her fingers felt strange, like warm oil mixed with rust. She swallowed hard, the metallic taste of it lingering in her throat though she had not touched her lips to the crimson stains.

She turned her attention to the guards who lay slumped nearby, their breaths slow and heavy with the effects of the drugged wine she had prepared. Their faces were slack, mouths agape in a parody of innocence. She moved quickly, her motions brisk and precise. With one swift motion, she pressed the first dagger into the hand of the nearest guard, smearing the blood along his fingers. The second dagger followed, its hilt shoved into the palm of the other man, her hands steady despite the tremor in her chest.

"See how guilt finds its mark," she murmured, her voice barely audible over the sound of her own breath. "The hand stained is the hand blamed."

The words carried no comfort. Her heart raced as she worked, her senses heightened to an unbearable degree. The faint rustle of her gown seemed deafening, the torch's flame a living, restless thing that hissed with every movement. The very air felt alive with accusation, and yet she moved as though possessed, her actions precise, practiced.

When she rose to her feet, she caught sight of her reflection in the polished surface of a silver basin. The blood on her hands gleamed darkly, its wet sheen catching the torchlight. She froze, staring at the image—a queen in her own mind, now reduced to a crimson-streaked spectre. The sight burned itself into her memory, and for a fleeting moment, she thought she could hear the blood itself, its faint trickle like the murmured curses of the dead.

"No," she whispered sharply, shaking her head as though to dislodge the thought. "This is the price of ambition. Nothing more."

She turned her back on the body, her movements quick and clipped as she extinguished the torch and stepped out of the chamber. The corridor seemed darker now, the torches along the walls guttering as though threatened by the night itself. She moved swiftly, her steps as silent as a shadow. Her breath misted before her in faint, spectral wisps, but she did not pause. The daggers were left behind, their work complete. Now, all that remained was to return to Macbeth.

The faintest sound met her ears—a knocking. She froze mid-step, her breath catching in her throat. The sound came again, louder this time, echoing through the castle like a thunderclap. It was steady, deliberate, and relentless, each strike reverberating through the stone.

Lady Macbeth quickened her pace, her heart pounding in time with the knocking. When she reached the chamber, she found Macbeth standing where she had left him, his face pale and his hands trembling. He turned toward her at the sound of her approach, his eyes wide with something that teetered between madness and despair.

"There's knocking at the gate," he said, his voice barely above a whisper. "Did you hear it?"

"I heard it," she replied, her tone sharp and controlled despite the tremor in her chest. She moved toward him, her hands brushing against his as though to ground him. "We must away. Wash the blood from your hands and play the host. The morning will come, and with it questions. We must have no answers."

Macbeth stared at her, his expression unreadable. "What have we done?" he murmured. His gaze flicked to his hands, still stained with blood. "The knocking... it will not stop."

Lady Macbeth gripped his arm tightly, her voice fierce. "Enough. The deed is done, and what's begun cannot be undone. Compose yourself."

But as the knocking continued, steady and insistent, Lady Macbeth felt her own composure slipping. The sound burrowed into her mind, relentless and accusing. Each strike seemed to echo with Duncan's name, with the weight of their crime. She turned toward the door, her heart hammering in her chest, her breath quickening.

The castle seemed to pulse with the sound, the air thickening, the shadows deepening. She glanced at Macbeth, her voice faltering as she spoke. "We must answer it."

Macbeth nodded, his face ashen, his movements slow and heavy. Together, they turned toward the door, the sound of the knocking growing louder, more insistent, as though it would never cease. Lady Macbeth straightened her spine, her expression hardening, but in her chest, the scorpion's sting of doubt curled tighter.

The knocking persisted, relentless and unyielding, driving them both toward an uncertain dawn.

ACT II SCENE 3

Groaning like a restless beast as the morning crept in, the castle was waking up. The faint light struggling to pierce through the mist that clung to its ancient walls. Within, silence reigned, broken only by the occasional murmur of servants stirring in their chambers. But at the gate, the persistent, echoing knock continued, relentless and unyielding as the sun brought forth the morning dew and a gentle mist.

The Porter stirred from his slumped position against the wall, groaning as if the very act of waking was an affront. His head throbbed with the remnants of last night's indulgence, the ale still heavy on his breath. He squinted at the door as if it might vanish under his gaze, but the knocking grew louder, more insistent. His limbs ached from the cramped night, and his thoughts—what few survived the fog in his skull—were tangled and unkind.

"Knock, knock," he muttered to himself, his voice gravelled by sleep and fermentation. "What, is this hell? Nay, too cold for that." A gust of wind shrieked through the gap beneath the door, and he shivered, drawing his cloak closer around him. "Hell hath fire. This place hath only damp and duty."

He staggered upright, joints creaking, and shuffled toward the door. His imagination, pickled and wild, had conjured all manner of sinners lining up at his gate—hypocrites in priests' robes, gluttons reeking of roasted fowl, lovers still slick with stolen trysts—all seeking the primrose path to the everlasting bonfire. He snorted at the thought.

"I'd make a poor devil's porter," he said aloud, fumbling with the iron bolt. "For even in hell they must sleep sometime."

The knocking grew more insistent. "Anon, anon!" he barked. "Hold thy horses and thine immortal soul!"

The bolt scraped open with a reluctant groan, and a slice of morning cut into the gloom.

There stood two men cloaked in mist, their breath billowing before them in clouds. One, stern-faced and resolute, was Macduff, nobleman of Fife, his expression drawn with urgency. Beside him lingered Lennox, ever the courtly observer, his eyes sharp beneath the feathered brim of his hat.

"Was it so late, friend," Macduff asked, stepping past the threshold, "that you lie abed so long?"

The porter gave a half-bow, clutching his head. "Faith, sir, we drank till the second cock, and mayhap the third. There is no hour safe from thirst when the wine is strong and the soul weaker still, and drink, sir, is a great provoker of three things."

Macduff raised an eyebrow. "And what does drink provoke, pray tell?"

The porter grinned, the gleam of mischief returning to his swollen eyes. "Marry, sir, three things it doth especially stir: nose-painting, sleep... and waterworks most unmusical." He gestured crudely to his groin and then to his blotched nose. "But chief among its mischiefs is lechery. It whets the appetite, aye, but dulls the blade. Drink is a jester—it invites the act, then steals the performance. It maketh brave men blush, and then sleep in shame."

Lennox laughed under his breath, but Macduff remained grave.

"I dare say it gave you the lie last night," Macduff said, eyeing the man's bleary face.

"That it did," the porter admitted cheerfully. "Straight to the throat, sir, bold as brass. But I flung it off me in the end. It had me by the legs for a time—aye, had me down—but I cast it out ere sunrise. One must fight for dignity where one can find it, no?"

A silence fell, brief but weighty, as Macduff's gaze travelled beyond the porter, into the shadowed depths of the castle. The warmth of jest faded from his face, replaced by a watchfulness honed by years of clan feuds and midnight betrayals.

"Is thy master stirring?"

The question seemed to still the air.

The porter scratched at his scalp, as though the answer were tucked behind his ear. "Not that I know, sir. I've heard no step nor stir since the night fell silent. Shall I fetch someone to rouse him?"

But Macduff was already moving, his boots striking stone with growing haste. Lennox followed, though his eyes lingered on the porter a moment longer, as if pondering whether jest was a shield or confession.

The porter watched them go, then turned back to the cold brazier, its embers almost dead. He sat once more on the stool, wrapping his cloak about him, alone with the echo of his own laughter and the faint memory of fire.

Outside, the wind scraped across the moors like claws on slate. And somewhere within the thick heart of the castle, where ambition had stirred and blood had spilled, a door had opened—and not just the one at the gate.

The courtyard was still shrouded in mist, the castle's towering walls looming like sentinels against the pale light. Macduff and Lennox moved swiftly toward the main entrance, their boots echoing on the stones. Inside, the air was thick with an eerie stillness, as though the castle itself held its breath. A servant emerged from a side corridor, his expression drawn with the exhaustion of too many tasks before dawn.

"Inform your lord that we are here to see King Duncan," Macduff ordered.

The servant nodded quickly and disappeared, his footsteps fading into the labyrinth of corridors. Macduff and Lennox exchanged a glance, their unease growing. There was something strange in the air—a tension that clung to the walls and seeped into their bones.

Macbeth approached, his cloak askew as if he had risen hastily. His face was a study in control, the mask of composure sitting too tightly on his bones.

Lennox offered a polite bow. "Good morrow, noble sir."

"Good morrow, both," Macbeth returned, though the warmth in his voice felt cooled, distant.

Macduff stepped forward. "Is the king stirring, worthy thane?"

Macbeth shook his head slowly, his eyes flickering, unreadable. "Not yet."

"He did command me to call timely upon him," Macduff said, glancing toward the hallway that led to Duncan's chamber. "I have almost slipped the hour."

"I'll bring you to him," Macbeth said, gesturing.

Macduff offered a wry smile. "I'm sure this is a welcome inconvenience for you—but still, it is one."

Macbeth's response came too quickly, too perfectly. "Joy tempers the bitter draught of duty... though not all labours leave the hands unstained." He turned and pointed to the heavy-latched door. "This is the door."

"I'll make so bold to call," Macduff said, moving forward. "It's my duty."

He stepped into the corridor and disappeared into the royal chamber, his boots receding into silence.

Lennox remained with Macbeth, rubbing his hands to warm them. "Is the king leaving today?"

Macbeth nodded. "He is—at least, that was his plan."

· · ·

As he approached the king's chamber, Macduff saw the sleeping guards, the door ajar, and smelled the tang of blood and death in the air. "Something is not right," he whispered to himself.

He pushed the door open, the faint creak of the hinges slicing through the silence like a blade. He stepped inside, the dim light revealing the outlines of the bed, the figure beneath its covers still and silent.

The scene seemed frozen, waiting for the next breath to shatter it.

He glanced toward a narrow lancet window where a pale sliver of light attempted to pierce the gloom. Macduff stepped into the dim chamber, his breath clouding faintly in the cool air. The heavy drapes hung still, their folds casting long shadows across the room. Duncan lay beneath the richly embroidered coverlet, his form unnaturally still. At first glance, the scene could have been mistaken for peaceful sleep, the serenity of the moment at odds with the unease that churned in Macduff's gut.

"Good morrow, my liege," Macduff called softly, his voice breaking the silence like a ripple on a still pond. He approached the bed with cautious steps, his instincts bristling at the unnatural quiet. His eyes scanned the room, taking in the unlit candelabra, the faint scent of lavender masking something darker—a metallic tang that caught in his throat.

He reached the bedside and placed a hand on the coverlet, intending to gently rouse the king. But the instant his fingers brushed the fabric, he froze. It was damp. Sticky. Cold.

His breath hitched, and he pulled the coverlet back with a swift motion. The sight beneath sent him reeling. Duncan lay sprawled, his white nightshirt soaked through with blood that had long since congealed. His throat gaped in a jagged slash, the wound stark against his pale skin. The sight seemed to pulse in the dim light, vivid and obscene.

"Dear God!" Macduff cried, stumbling backward. The words tore from him, raw and guttural, reverberating through the chamber. His knees buckled, but he caught himself against the edge of the bed, his eyes wide with horror.

. . .

Still in the courtyard, Lennox attempted small talk with Macbeth, whose stiffness he attributed to a night's revelry in courtship with the king. "The night was unruly," he said, voice low. "Where we lay, the chimneys were blown down, and strange lamentings were heard in the air—screams, sir, of death and despair. It was as if the heavens themselves were in rebellion."

Macbeth gave a slow nod, his eyes distant. "Aye. 'Twas a rough night."

Lennox shivered. "I can remember some frightening storms from my youth, but not so cursed as that."

Macbeth had no answer. Then—footsteps. Swift, halting, staggering.

Macduff reappeared in the hall, and his face was no longer that of a courtier but a man undone. His mouth moved soundlessly for a moment before the words burst forth in a voice torn raw.

"Oh, horror—unspeakable horror! There are no words fit to name it!"

Macbeth stepped forward, his tone urgent. "What is it you're saying? Speak plainly."

Lennox paled. "Mean you his majesty?"

Macduff raised a trembling hand. "Confusion has wrought its masterpiece. The most sacred life in this house has been violated—murdered. Our king—our sovereign, chosen by God—has been struck down in his sleep. His chamber is a tomb."

There was a sudden stillness, like breath drawn and held across the entire castle. It was Macbeth who first stirred, his voice barely rose above a whisper. "Are you saying... Duncan is dead?"

"Go and see for yourselves," Macduff said bitterly. "I dare not describe it—it is a sight that will ruin the eyes that behold it."

He staggered past them and emptied his breakfast on the cobbled stones of the castle's main path. Macbeth and Lennox swept past him, the great door groaning open behind them like a mouth unhinged in agony.

Macduff remained alone for but a moment before the enormity of what he had seen demanded action. He moved toward the great hall, shouting with a voice now changed—commanding, desperate.

"Wake! Sound the alarm bell! Treason and murder have crossed our threshold. Banquo! Donalbain! Malcolm! Rise! Cast off your sleep—it is but death's pale imitation—and face the truth! Come and see the face of doom! Rise from your beds as though from your graves, and stand against this horror!"

It seemed to take an eternity for the bell to ring, but when it sounded time stopped altogether. The bell rang out, cold and mournful, ushering in a new reality for those housed in the castle of Inverness, and the rest of Scotland.

Footsteps echoed overhead. The castle was stirring like a wounded beast.

"As from your graves rise up, and walk like sprites to countenance this horror!"

Lady Macbeth appeared, dishevelled and breathless, her nightgown clinging to her in the chill. Her face bore no makeup now—only the stark bone of her brow and the gleam of wide, questioning eyes.

"What's the business," she demanded, "that such a hideous trumpet calls to parley the sleepers of the house? Speak! Speak!"

Macduff turned to her, stricken. "O gentle lady," he said, with a gasp of pity, "the truth is not for your ears. To hear it spoken would wound the heart before the mind could grasp it."

Banquo arrived then, his hair tousled, his sword drawn in his trembling hand. "What is amiss?" he asked.

"Our royal master's murdered," Macduff said.

Lady Macbeth clutched at her throat. "No! What, in our house?"

Banquo's eyes darkened. "Too cruel anywhere," he said. "Dear Duff, I beg you, and say it is not so."

Macbeth returned, bloodless and dazed, Lennox behind him. Macbeth's voice, when it came, was thick with rehearsed grief.

"If only I had died an hour before this moment, I'd have lived in peace. From now on, nothing matters. Honour is gone. Grace is dead. Life's sweetness has drained away, and all that remains is bitter sediment."

Malcolm and Donalbain entered, pale and blinking. Donalbain's voice broke the thick silence. "What is amiss?"

Macbeth turned toward them, his voice like ice over black water. "You are in danger and do not yet know it. The spring, the head, the fountain of your bloodline is stopped. The very source of it is stopped."

Macduff stepped forward. "Your royal father's murdered."

Malcolm recoiled. "O, by whom?"

Lennox answered grimly. "It appeared to be his own guards. They were drenched in blood. We found their daggers, still wet, tossed beside them like butcher's tools. They stared blankly, stunned, as though caught in the middle of some dream or curse. None of us could trust them with our lives."

The murmur of voices in the corridor rose to a low roar as nobles and servants crowded together towards the king's chamber, their faces pale and drawn. The toll of the alarm bell reverberated through the castle, its mournful clang splitting the stillness of the morning. Macbeth stood at the edge of the gathering, his expression a mask of grief and fury, but beneath it, his thoughts churned like a tempest.

The guards still lay slumped outside Duncan's chamber, their hands streaked with blood, their daggers lying beside them like damning evidence. Lennox and Macduff stared down at them, their expressions heavy with disgust.

"Here lie the king's murderers," Macduff said, his voice hard with certainty. "Their treachery is written plainly in blood."

"Or planted by another hand," Lennox murmured, his gaze narrowing.

At that, Macbeth stepped forward, his movements deliberate and commanding. "These wretches deserve no trial, no questioning. They were entrusted with the king's safety, and they have betrayed that trust in the vilest way."

"Macbeth, wait—" Lennox began, but the words barely left his mouth before Macbeth drew his blade.

The first strike was swift and brutal, the dagger slicing the throat of the nearest guard. The man's eyes flew open, his drunken stupor giving way to a brief, choking gasp before his body went limp again. The second guard stirred, his movements sluggish, but Macbeth was upon him before he could rise. The blade struck true, silencing him in an instant.

The crowd recoiled, gasps and cries echoing through the hall. Macduff stepped forward, his hand going to his sword. "Macbeth! What have you done?"

Macbeth turned to him, his face flushed, his breathing ragged. "What needed to be done," he spat. "Do you think I could look upon these traitors, these vile betrayers of their sacred duty, and not act? They stole the life of our king! Their lives were forfeit the moment they raised their hands against him."

Macduff's gaze darkened, his jaw tightening. "And yet they could have spoken, answered for their crimes."

"What answer could they give that would undo what has been done?" Macbeth shot back, his voice rising. "Would you have me stand idle while the blood of our king cries out for justice?"

Lady Macbeth, who had been lingering near the doorway, stepped forward, her movements slow and deliberate. "My husband speaks the truth," she said, her voice calm but edged with steel. "Their guilt is evident, their punishment swift. Would you argue against such righteous fury?"

Macduff's hand fell from his sword, his expression grim but resigned. "No man can argue against justice, but we must tread carefully, for chaos will only breed more suspicion."

The crowd shifted uneasily, their whispers growing louder. Malcolm and Donalbain appeared at the edge of the gathering, their faces pale and stricken. Malcolm's eyes darted between the bloody daggers, the slumped guards, and the grim faces of the assembled nobles.

"Our father," Malcolm said softly, his voice trembling. "Is it true?"

Macduff turned to him, his expression softening. "I am sorry, my prince. It is true. Your father has been slain in the night."

Donalbain gasped, his hand flying to his mouth, but Malcolm's expression hardened, his shoulders straightening. "And who is to blame?"

Macbeth stepped forward, his bloodied blade still in hand. "The guards who lay at his door. Their weapons were found red with his blood, their hands stained with the proof of their treachery."

Malcolm's gaze lingered on Macbeth's blade, and a flicker of doubt passed over his face. "And now they are dead as well?"

"I saw to it myself," Macbeth said, his voice firm. "Their guilt was beyond question. Justice demanded swift action."

The younger prince, Donalbain, stepped closer to Malcolm, his voice low but urgent. "We are not safe here, brother. This place reeks of treachery."

Malcolm nodded, his expression grave. "You are right. Whoever has done this will not stop at our father."

Donalbain's voice dropped further, barely audible over the noise of the crowd. "Then we must leave. You to England, and I to Ireland. Separate, we are harder to find."

Malcolm hesitated, his gaze sweeping the room. "It will look like guilt."

"It will look like caution," Donalbain countered. "And we will return when the time is right."

Before Malcolm could respond, Lennox raised his voice, addressing the room. "We must decide what is to be done. The throne cannot sit empty, nor can this crime go unanswered."

The nobles murmured their agreement, their eyes drifting toward Macbeth, who stood tall and unyielding, his bloodied blade glinting in the dim light. Lady Macbeth moved to stand beside him, her expression unreadable but resolute.

"Duncan's death is a tragedy beyond words," Macbeth said, his voice steady and commanding. "But Scotland must not falter. We will mourn him, and we will seek out any who conspired in this vile act. But we must also look forward—to stability, to strength."

The murmurs grew louder, a mix of agreement and unease. Malcolm and Donalbain exchanged a glance, their silent decision solidifying. They slipped out of the room, unnoticed in the growing throng, their steps quick and purposeful.

The castle seemed to pulse with the rising tension, the air thick with suspicion and fear. As the crowd began to disperse, whispers spread like wildfire, each voice carrying a thread of doubt, of unease.

Macbeth sheathed his dagger, his gaze sweeping the room. His heart raced, but he forced his expression to remain calm, his mind already turning to the next step. The path to the throne was bloodstained, but it was clear.

Lady Macbeth placed a hand on his arm, her voice low. "The time will come to mourn. For now, you must lead."

Macbeth nodded, his lips pressing into a thin line. "I will."

ACT II SCENE 4

Fife castle stood alone atop a bluff, a bleak and brooding silhouette against the ashen sky. It was not a place of pomp, but of strength: a seat built for hard men and hard winters. Pale mist clung to the hills and valleys surrounding Macduff's stronghold, shrouding the earth in a woollen silence that seemed to muffle not only sound but thought. Here, news travelled slowly—by horse and by rumour—but even before the messengers arrived, something had shifted in the soil. The crows had taken to circling without landing. The hounds had refused their meat. And somewhere in the orchard, a tree had shed its blossom out of season, as if mourning. The courtyard at Fife was cloaked in a fog that did not lift with the sun, though the hour claimed to be well past dawn. Smoke clung to the eaves. Even the birdsong had withered into silence.

Ross stood near the outer steps, his breath a thin ghost in the air. By his side stood an old man dressed in the rough robes of a wandering monk, the hem muddied by the road, a rosary of dark wood swinging gently at his side. Yet behind him stood two men with cloaks drawn tight and swords beneath. A curious retinue for a lowly priest, though none remarked on it aloud. The old man's head was bald at the crown, with dark hair curling at the sides, and a neat, pointed beard framing a mouth that rarely betrayed what he thought. His eyes were steady, sharp — the kind that missed little, and remembered everything. A man who bore the mask of piety but carried within him the architecture of hidden truths. His voice, when he spoke, was low, measured, almost weary.

"Seventy years I have lived, and in that time I have seen war, famine, omens and horror enough to fill a scripture. But never have I known a night such as this last one. It makes a mockery of all I thought I understood."

Ross, who had ridden from Inverness without sleep, nodded gravely.

"You see it too, then? The heavens themselves seem shaken, disturbed by the sins of men. The sun should be risen by now, yet the sky clings to night like a widow to her mourning veil. It is as if the day itself is ashamed to show its face."

The old man tilted his head, eyes scanning the colourless sky. "It is unnatural," he said. "As unnatural as the deed that called it forth. On Tuesday last, they say, a falcon — proud, noble, soaring high above the trees — was struck and killed by an owl. A mere night-creature, hunting in daylight."

Ross glanced sideways, unsure if he heard parable or omen.

"And Duncan's horses," he said, his voice tightening. "Beautiful, swift creatures — the finest of their kind. They broke free of their stables, turned wild, fought their handlers... and then — God preserve us — turned on one another. They tore each other to pieces, as if madness had taken root in their blood."

The old man's eyes narrowed slightly. "So I have heard. And I believe it. The world turns upside down when kings are struck down in their sleep."

The old priest nodded slowly, folding his hands within his robes.

"Animals sense what men refuse to name. Blood in the air. Spirits disturbed."

Ross studied him. "You speak as though you expected such signs."

"Expected?" The old man allowed himself a thin smile, more rueful than amused. "No... but I was warned. In whispers. Old tongues, muttered by women who live too long and speak to fires and trees. You call them witches. The Church calls them heretics. Yet they have always had an eye for kingship—sometimes clearer than our own scribes."

Ross's brow furrowed. "You mean the women Macbeth met on the moor?"

"So he told Duncan's men," the priest said, gaze distant. "But their tongues foretold more than just his rise. The old faith lingers in the hills. It knows when the crown will pass hands, and whether it is taken or given."

Ross stepped back slightly, uncertain. "And does the Church pay such riddles any mind?"

"We mind what men believe," the priest said quietly. "That is the first duty of shepherds. Macbeth is a man of piety, outwardly. He gives coin to the shrines. He keeps the rites. But the soul... the soul may smile while the hands are red."

Ross stared. "You believe he did it."

The old priest did not answer. He turned instead to look skyward, where the mist clung stubbornly to the horizon like ash refusing the wind.

"There are those within the Abbey at Dunkeld who already write his name into their prayers," he said softly. "The world moves quickly to bless a victor. But Heaven waits a little longer. It listens."

Ross felt a chill that had nothing to do with the weather.

"The bells may ring for Macbeth," the priest continued, "but the stones beneath our feet have not yet spoken."

Just then, footsteps echoed on the flagstones. Macduff strode into the courtyard, his face pale but resolute.

Ross greeted him. "How does the world stand now, my lord?"

Macduff gave him a long look. "Surely you see it for yourself."

Ross hesitated, then asked, "Is it known yet who committed the murder?"

Macduff nodded grimly. "The guards — those Macbeth slew — are held to blame."

Ross frowned. "What purpose could they have in such a bloody act?"

"They were bribed," Macduff said flatly. "Bought. And the king's two sons — Malcolm and Donalbain — fled before sunrise. Their escape has drawn suspicion squarely upon them."

Ross's face darkened. "Still against nature. To rise by slaying one's own blood — ambition that devours its very source. Then I suppose... the crown will pass to Macbeth?"

Macduff's jaw tensed. "It already has. He's ridden to Scone to be crowned."

Ross's eyes narrowed. "And the king's body?"

"Taken to Colmekill," Macduff replied, his voice quieter. "The sacred place where the old kings lie. He will rest among them now."

Ross's hand twitched at his side. "Will you go to Scone?"

Macduff shook his head. "No, cousin. I go home. To Fife."

Ross inclined his head, though his voice carried a thread of doubt. "Then I'll go on to Scone."

Macduff's tone sharpened ever so slightly. "Well, may you find things as they should be. But I pray we do not find our new robes fit less comfortably than our old."

The old priest remained still, his hands once again folded into his sleeves. Then, in a voice almost casual, he said:

"A shame, what the king's sons have done. But blood will tell, as the ancients say. It runs hot in youth... and sometimes boils over."

Ross blinked, startled. "You believe it was Malcolm and Donalbain now? You said—"

The old man smiled, patient as stone. "The world moves quickly, Master Ross. Faster than horses, faster than truth. It is not for men like us to quarrel with the tide."

One of the guards behind him shifted — a small step, a flicker of disquiet, like a hound bristling at something unseen. The priest did not turn, but only tilted his head slightly.

The guard froze.

Then the priest stepped forward, placing two fingers in blessing upon Ross's brow — a gesture more political than holy.

"God's blessings go with you," he said softly, his smile lingering, "and with those that would make good of bad, and friends of foes."

And then he turned, his robes whispering against the stone as he passed into the mist, the guards falling in silently behind him.

ACT III

ACT III SCENE 1

Banquo stood beneath the eaves of the upper court, where banners swayed lazily in the breeze and the stones still smelled faintly of rain. The sky was a dull silver, neither storming nor fair, and he watched it as though it might speak some truth aloud.

He spoke softly, to no one but the empty air.

"He has it all now—Glamis, Cawdor... king. Just as the witches said."

His fingers twitched at his side, the habitual ghost of reaching for his sword.

"And yet I fear... he played it foul. No honest blade wins a crown so swiftly—not when Duncan slept so soundly, and woke not at all."

His gaze dropped to the flagstones, where a dark patch stained the edge of the well—a memory that would not wash away, though the servants tried.

"Still... the prophecy was true. And if it spoke true for him, might it not speak true for me?"

He looked up again, eyes narrowing.

"They said his seed would not wear the crown. That I would be father to kings. If truth springs from their mouths, let it fall for me as well."

He paused, then shook his head sharply—as though clearing a mist from his thoughts.

"Enough. Hope is a hungry beast, and I have ridden with it long enough."

A trumpet sounded within the palace, and the doors opened in regal flourish. King Macbeth emerged, crowned and cloaked, flanked by Lady Macbeth in emerald and sable. Their train followed—Lennox, Ross, and other lords, dressed in colours bright as bruises.

Macbeth's gaze found Banquo at once, and he extended his arms with courtly warmth. "Here's our chief guest."

Lady Macbeth offered a smile like a polished mask. "Had he been forgotten, the feast would've felt misshapen—as though missing a limb."

Macbeth stepped forward. "Tonight, we hold a solemn supper, and your presence is requested. No, more than that—required."

Banquo bowed, his tone light but formal. "Your Majesty need only name it. My loyalty is bound fast, with ties no hand can cut."

"Will you ride this afternoon?" Macbeth asked, a little too casually.

"Aye," said Banquo. "Enough to pass the time 'til supper. If my horse proves lazy, I'll borrow an hour or two from the dark."

"We'd hoped to consult you at council," Macbeth said. "Your mind's ever been sharp and well-tempered. But we'll save it for tomorrow."

He paused. "You ride far?"

"Far enough to loosen the stiffness from the saddle," Banquo replied. "But not so far I won't be back in time to toast you."

Macbeth smiled. "Fail not our feast."

"My lord," Banquo said with a faint incline of the head, "I would not."

Macbeth's tone shifted, cool as the morning wind. "We hear our bloody cousins now take shelter in England and Ireland—confessing nothing, only spreading lies."

"Strange tales reach every corner of the isle," Banquo said. "But truth has a way of bleeding through, if you let it."

Macbeth tilted his head. "We'll speak more of that tomorrow. For now—hie you to horse. Goes Fleance with you?"

"He does," said Banquo. "The boy's grown restless with stone walls and sermons. The road is better school."

Macbeth nodded. "Then may your horses be swift and your return swifter still."

He stepped forward, lowering his voice slightly. "Tell me true, Banquo—do you ever wonder if it might've been you?"

Banquo raised an eyebrow. "On the throne?"

Macbeth smiled thinly. "Stranger things have happened. The witches named you the root of kings."

There was a flicker behind Banquo's eyes—an old flame relit.

"I wonder," he said, "if any man would've done different in your place. Had the chance. The will. The stars overhead."

Macbeth's gaze sharpened. "Is that so?"

Banquo gave a small, knowing smile. "You did what had to be done. I don't judge you for it. But I never forget what's been promised me."

Banquo's gaze swept the horizon absently, though there was little to see. The fog had begun to lift, but its memory still veiled the landscape. He cleared his throat—not loudly, but with just enough weight to signal thought that had been brewing. His eyes flicked sideways. "It occurs to me now, your nobility was born not only of battlefields... but from fire. Fifty souls, if I remember the tale. A hall consumed. Strange what smoke can crown."

Macbeth's fists tightened imperceptibly by side, hovering near the dagger he kept ever at his side, his utensil for eating and anything else that required a blad to hand. His smile, when it came, was thin as a knife's edge. "Banquo, you should know, having been warmed by that blaze yourself. Ash cools with time, though some seem eager to rake through it."

"Not I," Banquo said easily. "But I do wonder. The boy you keep close—your squire, your quiet shadow. Is he not the seed of that same flame? The son of the man burned? Still you keep him beneath your roof, at your table, at your side. Curious choice."

"He is like a son to me," Macbeth said after a beat. "Loyal, useful, quiet. All qualities prized in a world where loyalty... grows scarce." Macbeth looked straight into the eyes of his brother in arms then. Banquo returned the gaze, unflinching, then chuckled softly.

"Aye. And yet my own family tree grows strong on parchment. Penned quickly, perhaps, but it has taken root nonetheless. Clergy and court alike seem eager to water it."

Macbeth turned to look at him, the smile still there, but colder now. "And you trust such ink? Your lineage written with a scribe's eager hand, still wet from flattery and fear? That tree may grow tall, Banquo—but its roots are shallow."

"Perhaps," Banquo replied, his tone still genial. "But it was written with a feather. Yours—with steel."

Macbeth did not answer immediately. The wind stirred again, lifting the ends of their cloaks like unseen hands. At last, he said, almost idly, "Steel is truth, when all is said."

"And steel kills truth," Banquo murmured, "when all are dead."

The words hung behind him like a banner, limp but unmistakable.

Macbeth watched him go. The muscles in his jaw flexed. His fingers strayed to the chain at his throat, where the amber talisman lay hidden beneath royal velvet. Within it, the scorpion waited—poised, patient, deadly.

"He wears prophecy like armour," Macbeth murmured. "Even now he dares to name his sons kings."

In his mind's eye, Banquo was no longer his dearest friend, no longer brother-in-arms. He was a mirror. A rival, coiled and watching. Waiting to strike.

"Let every man be master of his time 'til seven," Macbeth said aloud. "Let the feast come, and let the welcome be sweet."

He turned away from the courtyard, voice colder now, flint on steel.

"Until then... God be with you."

The court filed out, their laughter echoing faintly through the stone, leaving Macbeth alone with the flicker of torches and the hissing of something unseen beneath his skin.

Banquo's departing steps echoed in the hall like a fading heartbeat—measured, noble, and unknowing. Macbeth watched him go, his eyes narrowing not in farewell but in calculation, as though watching the drift of a shadow across a sundial and knowing dusk would fall sooner than expected. He turned to his assembled thanes with a courtly smile. "Let every man be master of his time till seven at night," he said. "To make society the sweeter welcome, we will keep ourself till supper-time alone. While then, God be with you."

The nobles bowed and withdrew, the rustle of fine wool and iron-trimmed leather retreating through the stony corridors. Left behind in the silence, Macbeth's mask slipped. He exhaled once—short and sharp—as if purging the breath he had held in Banquo's presence.

Macbeth turned to his armiger who was lingering at the edge of the chamber. "Tell me—are those men I sent for still waiting?"

"Yes, my lord," the youth replied, bowing almost imperceptibly. "They're just outside the gates."

"Bring them before us."

As the youth departed, Macbeth drifted to the centre of the chamber. The air hung heavy, oppressive with the stifled musk of burning peat and old ambition. He spoke now not to any ear but to the shadow that paced behind his own thoughts:

To be thus is nothing... but to be safely thus.

The throne, recently acquired, felt like a blade turned sideways beneath his skin—he sat upon it, but it cut him still.

Our fears in Banquo stick deep...

117

He loomed large in Macbeth's mind: Banquo, the warrior with eyes like burnished steel and a conscience chiselled from granite. His calm defied suspicion, his honour incapable of fracture, and worst of all, his blood—cursed with prophecy—flowed in the veins of that silent-eyed boy, Fleance.

If that prophecy holds true—if Banquo's line is to inherit the crown—then I've damned my soul for nothing. It was for them I killed Duncan, for them I broke my peace and gave my eternal soul to the enemy of mankind. All of it, so his children might rule?

He pressed his fists together, as if trying to crush fate between his palms.

No. No—I will not let it be. Come then, Fate. Step into the ring. I'll meet you blow for blow, and fight this to the end.

A knock—barely audible—answered his cry. He turned, eyes kindling.

"Who's there?"

His armiger returned, two figures in his wake. They entered with the cautious gait of men unaccustomed to palaces, their shoulders bent not by age but by the stoop of hunger and the habit of being overlooked. The first was lean, almost wolfish, with a scar cut through one cheek like a lightning strike; the second broader, slower in movement but with eyes that burned from a lifetime of resentment.

"Go to the door," Macbeth told the lad, "and stay there till we call."

Alone with the two, Macbeth let silence steep. The fire in the grate spat softly.

Macbeth paced before the hearth, his silhouette cast long and fractured by firelight. The two men stood before him—one tall and lean, face furrowed like a ploughed field, the other broader, stooped, hands clasped tight as though wringing something that wouldn't come clean.

"It was just yesterday we spoke," Macbeth said, his voice calm, measured. "Have you thought since then on what I told you?"

"We have," said the taller man, gravel-voiced. "Aye, we've thought."

"Then you remember," Macbeth continued, stepping closer, "it was not I who brought ruin to your lives. It was Banquo—he who played the noble thane by day and crushed you in court behind closed doors. You thought me blind to it, but I showed you—how he turned the law against you, how he chose whom to favour and whom to cast aside. You remember?"

The shorter man's jaw clenched. "I remember."

"Good," said Macbeth. "Because I need to know what lives in you now. Is your patience so holy, so harmless, that you would kneel and pray for the man who bowed your backs and drained your bloodline of hope?"

The leaner of the two scoffed softly. "Pray for him?" He shook his head. "He seized my land. Said I owed the grain to the crown. Sent men to strip the storehouse while my children cried for bread. I was called a thief on my own soil."

The second man stepped forward, voice quieter but edged with steel. "And me—I fought for him. Took a pike through the thigh at Macdonwald's line. When the fighting ended, I asked for a place at court. He looked me up and down like I was dirt with a voice, and told me my manners weren't fit for royal service."

He looked Macbeth dead in the eye. "I watched lads who never saw battle sit at the king's table while I dragged a lame leg back to a cottage that leaks and a mother too blind to tell if it's day or night."

There was a pause—heavy, close as breath.

"You made it plain," the first said. "We understand."

"I went further," Macbeth pressed. "Now, I ask again—can you let this go? Is your patience so dominant, so pious, that you'll pray for the man who broke your backs and beggared your kin? Banquo, who stands smiling while you crouch beneath the lash he ordered?"

There was a beat, heavy as a funeral drum.

"We are men, my liege," the scarred one answered.

"Aye," Macbeth said, his voice soft, almost sympathetic, "and so are hounds and greyhounds, mongrels, curs. They all share the name of 'dog', yet they differ—some are swift, some are sly, some stand sentinel while others hunt. So too with men."

Macbeth nodded slowly. "I ask you now: do you want to lie down like house-curs, or rise as wolves. I offer you a place in the king's regard."

They exchanged a look. No words, just the flicker of recognition between two men who had lived too long without being seen.

"You already know," said the second man. "Why else are we here?"

Macbeth smiled, dark and thin. "Then hear me plain. Banquo is your enemy. He is mine too—and far more dangerous than most know. Every moment he draws breath, he endangers the crown I wear. And I cannot strike at him directly, not without drawing blood from hands I still need loyal."

He paused, letting the firelight catch the glint of determination in his eyes.

"That is why I come to you. This business must be handled quietly, and it must be done tonight. Away from the palace. No stumbles, no witnesses. And it must not stop with Banquo."

He stepped closer, his voice dropping to a growl.

"His son rides with him. The boy must fall too."

The taller man raised his chin. "That your command, then?"

"It is," Macbeth replied. "Strike them both. Leave no root behind. The throne is mine by blood and blade, and I will not have it stolen by the ghost of a prophecy."

The two men nodded, grim and slow.

"We'll do it," said the lean one.

The taller man gave a curt nod. "We'll do it."

The other hesitated, then added, "Though our lives—"

Macbeth raised a hand—graceful, dismissive. He didn't look at them as he spoke, his gaze fixed on the darkening embers of the hearth.

"Your spirits shine through you," he said, almost warmly, as if their oath were a small comfort in a troubled hour. "Within this hour, at most, I'll send word—where to place yourselves, when to strike. I've a man close to Banquo who'll see them out. The time will be perfect."

He turned then, eyes gleaming with that strange mix of control and fever.

"It must be tonight. And it must not trace back here—I need a clean break from this house. No loose ends, no stumbles. Banquo must fall…"

A breath, and then colder:

"…and with him, his son. Fleance walks with him—shadow to his father's ambition. I cannot have one without the other. The boy must embrace the fate of that dark hour."

He stepped back, voice dropping low.

"Resolve yourselves apart. I'll come to you anon."

The two men bowed and left in silence, the echo of their departure swallowed by the stone. Macbeth stood alone in the gathering dusk, his face half-lit by firelight, half-lost in shadow.

He could not feel safe—not truly, not while Banquo yet drew breath.

The man's presence gnawed at the edges of Macbeth's calm like ivy splitting stone. There was in Banquo a kind of quiet nobility, unshaken even beneath the weight of prophecy. He bore the touch of destiny like a native thing, not a burden. That royalty of nature—it reigned in him as surely as any crown. He dared much, yes, but it was not rashness; his courage moved in lockstep with a mind sharpened by caution. Of all men, Macbeth feared him most.

And beneath that fear stirred something colder: humiliation. In Banquo's silence, he heard rebuke. Just as Mark Antony once quailed before the cool command of Caesar, so Macbeth felt himself diminished beneath the shadow of the friend who once called him brother.

He remembered the moor, the sting of rain and the witches' voices curling like smoke. How Banquo had scoffed when they named Macbeth king—king!, as though it were a jest—and then, like one seer reading another's truth, asked what they had to say for him. And they had answered: not for himself, but for his blood. They hailed him father to a line of kings.

And what of Macbeth? A crown had been set upon his brow, but it grew no roots. A hollow gift. A circlet of gilt with no lineage to bind it. They had given him a sceptre—but it was barren, cold in his grip, unwarmed by the flesh of any son to inherit it.

No son of his would rise. The only child in his house was not his own.

Lulach, Seyton. The name was changed, but the blood was not.

Gruoch's son. Gille's son. The boy spared the fire and sealed by promise. Seyton bore his name now, served at his side, a page wrapped in the illusion of future blood. Banquo's blood will out before mine.

And it was not prophecy alone that crowned Banquo's line. No—they watched him too. Those tonsured men who wrote future history. The priests. The monks. The ink-stained fingers of the Abbey scribes. Those who anoint with oil and parchment. Already they chronicled Banquo in their ledgers, praised his piety, his steadfastness, his humble loyalty to a throne for which his children were to be groomed. If Macbeth was born of storms and shadow, Banquo would be the man canonised in the quiet, in candlelight, long after both were dust.

And so the threat was twofold—witchcraft and scripture. Fate and faith. Blades and books. Was this the price of all he had done? He had murdered Duncan—murdered sleep itself—poisoned his peace and sold the last ember of his soul to the devil's ledger. And for what? For Banquo's seed to wear the crown?

No. No, rather fate itself could come down into the lists, and he would meet it blade for blade. He would not be an instrument for another man's legacy. He would not be the path Banquo's line walked to power.

Let destiny raise its standard—he would strike it down.

. . .

The stone corridors of the castle swallowed the sound of the murderers' footsteps. Macbeth lingered a moment longer in the hall, the weight of resolve still settling in his bones. Then he turned and slipped into the quiet of their chamber, where shadows gathered like confidants.

Lady Macbeth stood near the window, the last grey light of evening tracing the hard angle of her cheek. She did not turn when he entered, only spoke—calm, assured.

"Excited, for the 'morrow's feast? I have been making preparations befitting a king." She smiled at this, this being their first royal banquet.

"Aye," he said. "They'll be ready."

She turned then, her eyes catching the fading light like twin shards of polished jet. "The hall is near set," she said, voice low. "The goblets laid, the boards dressed. I've had the serving lasses scrub the stone twice over. Still, it smells of soot."

He raised a brow. "Soot?"

She gave a small, humourless shrug. "Nothing. Ghosts of other fires, perhaps."

A silence stretched between them.

She crossed to him slowly, the heavy hem of her gown whispering across the floor. She said nothing at first, only reached up and touched the small amber talisman that hung at his throat. Inside it, suspended in its resin coffin, the curled black body of the scorpion stared out like a fossilised secret.

"I remember when you first wore this," she said softly, her fingers brushing its surface. "You said it calmed the storm in you. That it reminded you to be still. To strike only when the time was right."

He gave a humourless half-smile. "It reminded me that poison needn't rush. That patience has its own venom."

Her hand lingered a moment longer, then dropped. "And now?"

He met her gaze. "Now it reminds me that kings must kill more than once."

She stepped closer, close enough that he could smell the clove oil she sometimes pressed behind her ears, a habit left over from the colder months in Moray.

"Are you still a man of your word?" she asked.

His brow furrowed. "In what sense?"

She paused. "You made promises once—before crowns, before prophecy. Before... the night of the fire."

Macbeth's jaw tightened, but he said nothing.

"That hall was full," she said, her voice even but distant. "Fifty souls. Gille among them. You told me the door would be fastened only after Lulach was safely gone."

"He was safely gone," he said. "Besides, he is called Seyton now."

"I know. But still, I wake thinking I see his shadow outlined in flame."

The scorpion swung slightly on its chain as he breathed in. "And you regret it, Gruoch?"

Her voice was quiet. "I remember it."

She turned back to the window, her gaze reaching out over the stone courtyard, now gilded in the last threads of dusk. "This is the first time I have hosted as queen. Every detail must be perfect. Every goblet, every cut of meat. They will be watching. We earned this place—but not all forget how it was bought."

His tone darkened. "Let them remember. Let them choke on it."

She smiled faintly. "They won't. Not if the wine flows fast enough."

A silence fell again, less tense now—more like the stillness before a long night's vigil. The feast to come pressed down upon them both in different ways: hers full of ceremony, his full of consequence.

Outside, the first distant notes of preparation drifted through the corridor—laughter, the clink of goblets, the wheeze of pipes tuning for the feast.

He turned away from the window. "We should go."

She nodded, moving toward the door. Then paused.

"There'll be ghosts enough tonight, I'm sure," she said. "Let us not wear them on our faces."

She left the chamber. Macbeth glimpsed the pale youth just outside the door—reliable and comforting, like the echo of a promise. Macbeth had come to love that boy, or man… whatever he was. But he was an empty vessel, and that was neither his fault nor the boy's. Could he blame the mother for that? They shared the same deathly dignity, the ferocity of a wight and the grace of a frosted rose. In a rare moment

126

of affection, he saw Lady Macbeth touch the palm of her hand to the youth's soft cheek for a short moment before she turned down the corridor. The youth's face remained utterly unchanged. Impassive. Then his dark eyes met Macbeth's—piercing, loyal. The gaze of a dagger, had it the instruments of vision. The door closed quietly, leaving Macbeth alone in the chamber.

"It is concluded," he muttered. "Banquo, thy soul's flight, if it find heaven, must find it out tonight."

ACT III SCENE 2

The hall lay shrouded in a silence so heavy it felt as though even the stone walls bore the weight of it. Shadows crept across the floors and walls, spilling like ink from the jagged angles of the flickering candelabras. Lady Macbeth stood at the window, her slender figure framed by the storm-laden sky. The glass was cold beneath her palm, and beyond it, the night howled with a ferocity that made the walls seem fragile by comparison. As she stared out into the courtyard below, movement caught her eye—a pair of figures on horseback passing beneath the archway. Banquo, unmistakable in posture, rode with his son beside him, the boy's dark cloak whipping behind him like a shadow unfurling. The gates creaked as they closed behind them, and the courtyard swallowed the sound of hoofbeats.

She watched them vanish down the hill.

Her reflection in the glass startled her—eyes dark with sleeplessness, skin pale and drawn. This was not the face of the woman who had boldly whispered murder into her husband's ear, who had stoked the fires of his ambition until they consumed them both. This face, lined with worry, belonged to someone else. Someone weaker.

She pressed her hand harder against the window, as though the pressure might anchor her, might force her back into the role she had claimed with such conviction. I am queen now. This is what I wanted. This is what we wanted. But the words felt hollow, the echo of a distant truth.

The sound of her own breath filled her ears, harsh and shallow. The air in the chamber was close, oppressive. She turned from the window, her movements abrupt, her silk gown whispering against the flagstones. The fire in the hearth burned low, the embers casting a faint red glow that seemed to pulse like a dying heart. She shivered, though the air by the hearth was warm compared to the window.

Where was he? Macbeth had been absent from her side more often of late, retreating into the labyrinth of his thoughts, the shadow of his own ambition darkening his every expression. He had always been a man of intensity, but now that intensity frightened her. It was as if something had taken root within him, twisting and growing beyond her reach. She could no longer see the man she had loved, the man she had burned for, beneath the mask of his resolve.

Her hand drifted to her throat, fingers brushing the jewels that adorned her neck. They were heavy, these trappings of power, and she could not shake the feeling that they were more a noose than a crown.

"Why do you hide from me?" she whispered, the words spoken to the empty room. The sound of her voice startled her, and she pressed her lips together, as though silence could reclaim the vulnerability she had let slip. "We've gained nothing," she murmured. "Spent all, won less. What joy lies in the crown, when every breath we take beneath it is watched? It's safer, perhaps, to be the thing we destroy than to live hollow-eyed in fear of its return."

The door creaked open behind her, and she turned sharply, her heart lurching. A servant lingered in the doorway, cap in hand, eyes cast low.

"Banquo," she said, masking her thoughts beneath cool poise. "He has left the court—where is he riding?"

The servant bowed his head. "Only for the afternoon, madam. He rides the southern road with his son. But he said he'll return before nightfall. For the feast."

She nodded, almost absently. "Tell the king I would speak with him... when it pleases him."

The servant turned to go—only to nearly collide with Macbeth, who entered just as the boy reached the threshold.

There was a pause. Macbeth's hand reached lightly to the boy's shoulder.

"Seyton—your hands must also avail the deed. The owl has eyes tonight," he murmured, voice low and thick as fog. "The snake is in the heather. Tell those who wait: the road bends where the pines begin. No noise. No trace. See it is done."

The quiet servant gave a near-imperceptible nod and vanished down the corridor.

Lady Macbeth had not noticed. She turned quickly. "There you are, my lord. Why do you walk alone, keeping such mournful company as your own thoughts? You chew on shadows as though they were substance. These thoughts should have died with the men you took them from. What's done is done."

Macbeth halted near the hearth, staring into the low flames, his profile drawn and restless.

"We've scorched the snake," he said. "But not killed it."

He turned toward her, his voice darkening.

"She'll heal—hide her venom beneath smooth scales—and strike again. Our malice hasn't ended the danger. It's made it quieter. Hungrier."

He moved past her.

"Let the world crack. Let heaven fall and hell open its mouth. I care not—so long as I no longer eat in fear or sleep with these... these ghosts tearing at my mind."

He pressed a hand briefly to his temple.

"Every night they come. Not the witches now—but dreams. Dreams with Duncan's eyes. Dreams with blood I can't wash off. They make my waking worse than any blade."

Lady Macbeth stood still, watching him. She had not heard him speak of Duncan in days.

"Duncan," Macbeth continued, "sleeps well. He's past it now. No knives, no poison, no uprising, no whispered treachery can touch him where he lies. We sent him to peace... and we won none for ourselves."

A quiet moment passed.

She stepped closer, laying a hand on his arm, her touch soft but firm.

"Come now," she said gently. "My love. Smooth those furrows from your brow. You must greet your guests tonight with light in your eyes, not thunder. Let them see the king—not the shadow of the man who took the crown."

Lady Macbeth's hand lingered at his arm, smoothing down the tension in his muscles like one would a snarling dog.

"Come now," she said again, more softly. "Gentle my lord. sleek over your rugged looks." She surprised herself at her flirtatiousness, for she felt nothing truly but a lonely desire that any man other than her husband could serve her. The cold realisation that her husband—once fire and fury—was now something else entirely. A man sealed in amber, unreachable. Her voice carried on, practised and smooth: "Be bright tonight—charming. Let the crown sit lightly upon your brow, and let no one see the storm behind your eyes."

Macbeth turned his gaze to her. Something flickered there—affection, perhaps, or something less nameable. His voice softened.

"I shall, my love. And you too, I pray—match my mask with one of your own. Especially with Banquo."

She stilled slightly at the name. She was fond of Banquo, he was to be the guest of honour tonight, yet she felt uneasy as her husband mentioned his name.

"Offer him honour. Smile at him. Let your eyes and tongue both grant him grace. It is safer, for now, that we gild our thoughts in flattery, and bathe our guilt in shallow courtesies. These are the waters in which honour must be washed clean."

She met his gaze.

"You must let this go."

But Macbeth stepped away, one hand rising to the scorpion talisman at his throat, hidden beneath the folds of his mantle. His fingers pressed the amber shape as though to draw venom from it.

"O, full of scorpions is my mind, dear wife," he meant merely to speak those words, yet they gushed from his throat in a strangled scream. "You know that Banquo lives. And Fleance." He was breathless after this pained utterance, his voice rasping. His hand flew to his throat as if to claw the swarm back down, but it was too late—the sting of it was everywhere. Behind his eyes. Beneath his ribs. They skittered through him, these thoughts—sharp-tailed, sleepless, countless.

She frowned slightly. "They are flesh and blood, not phantoms. And nature's copy isn't eternal."

"There's comfort in that," he said, trying to regain his composure. "Because flesh can be undone."

He crossed to the window, where the light had begun to fade into the smoky hue of approaching dusk.

"Be glad tonight," he said, without turning back. "Before the bat wings from the chapel eaves, before the beetle drones his drowsy song beneath Hecate's eye—there shall be done a deed."

She came a step closer. "What deed?"

He looked at her over his shoulder. His smile did not reach his eyes.

"Be innocent of the knowledge, dearest heart," he said, voice warm but edged. "Until you can applaud it."

He turned to the window again, voice rising with the weight of invocation.

"Come, sealing night. Bind the eyes of daylight with your black scarf. Let your invisible and blood-soaked hand rip apart the thread that ties me to this fear."

Outside, a crow rose, its wings dark against the thickening sky, cutting across the last bruised edge of sun.

"The light thickens," Macbeth murmured. "The crow flies to the rooky wood. And all good things of the day begin to droop and doze... while night's black agents wake and stalk."

Lady Macbeth watched him. There was something in his posture—straighter, colder, solitary.

"You wonder at my words," he said, turning to her again. "But stay silent. Evil, once begun, only grows stronger by its own motion."

He extended a hand.

"So, I pray you—walk with me."

She placed her hand in his, and together they stepped from the chamber, their shadows flickering across the stone as the last light slipped away.

ACT III SCENE 3

Ancient, silent, listening. The forest stretched endlessly, its shadows weaving a tapestry of despair beneath the cold, indifferent light of the waxing moon. The branches above twisted like the gnarled fingers of old crones, their bare tips scraping at the night sky. The air was thick with the scent of damp earth and rotting leaves, a cloying perfume that clung to the skin and seeped into the lungs. Beneath the canopy, all was still, save for the faint rustle of unseen creatures and the distant call of a lone owl.

Two figures crouched among the undergrowth, their silhouettes barely distinguishable from the twisted trunks around them. The murderers had taken their positions with the practiced stillness of predators, their forms tense and coiled like vipers ready to strike. Both men were accustomed to hunting and even poaching, as desperation had led them before to acts of moral ambiguity. Yet within them, the stillness was a lie. Their thoughts churned, each one caught in the grip of a silent struggle.

The first man, a wiry figure with scarred features and eyes that darted like a trapped animal's, tightened his grip on the dagger at his side. His breath came shallow and quick, the weight of their task pressing down on him like the suffocating air of the forest. He glanced at his companion, his unease clear in the taut lines of his face.

"Why must it be this way?" he whispered, his voice barely audible over the rustling leaves. "The man is no enemy of ours. What debt do we owe the crown that we must soil our hands for its sake?"

The second man, broader and more weathered, his face shadowed beneath a hood, turned to him sharply. "You question it now?" he hissed, his tone low and harsh. "You took the coin, same as me. Do you think we'll see mercy if we balk at the deed? Besides, he wronged us both and we know it."

The first man's gaze dropped to the forest floor, his fingers loosening on the hilt of his weapon. "Coin is cold comfort," he muttered. "It won't wash the blood from my hands."

The third figure, a lanky man with a face hollowed by years of hardship, spoke at last, his voice rough and resigned. "Blood's already on us," he said simply. "What's one more stain?"

Then a third figure emerged from the shadows. He appeared in the glade as if drawn by the scent of blood. He was younger than the others. Slighter. His hood was drawn low, and he moved with a fluid, silent grace that made him seem more shadow than man. No name passed his lips.

"Who sent you?" asked the first, his voice low.

"Macbeth," said the newcomer.

That was all. But the way he said it—the certainty of it—left no doubt.

The second man nodded to the first. "He needs no testing. He knows the work. And the work knows him."

The scar-faced man nodded, "He knows what's to be done, and when. No cause to question."

The third man, who in truth was little more than a boy, settled in-between the other two, silent and taut as a bowstring. Any previous doubts had dissipated with his sudden arrival.

The silence that followed was heavy, filled with the unspoken weight of their collective guilt. Above them, the trees swayed in a sudden breeze, their branches groaning as though in protest. The first man shivered, his unease deepening.

"This forest," he murmured, glancing around nervously. "It feels… wrong. Malevolent, somehow."

The second man let out a bitter laugh, his teeth flashing in the darkness. "Superstitious fool," he said, though his own voice trembled with something he would not name. "The forest knows nothing. It's the living we have to fear."

But even as he spoke, the shadows seemed to shift, their edges sharpening, their forms more distinct. The murderers huddled closer together, their eyes scanning the gathering darkness as though expecting the forest itself to rise against them.

The sound of hoofbeats broke the stillness, faint at first but growing steadily louder. The men stiffened, their hands moving to their weapons, their breathing shallow. The path before them, winding and narrow, stretched into the gloom, its edges softened by the pale light of the moon. From its depths, the figures of Banquo and his son emerged, their forms ghostly in the half-light.

Banquo rode at the front, his head held high, his cloak billowing behind him like a shadow. Fleance followed closely, his smaller figure dwarfed by the horse he rode. The boy's face was turned upward, his expression intent as he whispered to his father, though his words were lost to the distance.

The first man swallowed hard, his grip tightening on his dagger once more. "It's a boy," he muttered, his voice filled with quiet horror. "We're to kill a boy?"

"Silence," the third man growled, his voice like the snap of a branch beneath heavy boots. "We do what we must."

But the first man's hands trembled, the weight of the task sinking into him like a stone in deep water. His breath came faster, louder, and the second man turned on him with a ferocity born of desperation.

"If you falter now," he snarled, "it will be your blood spilled alongside theirs."

The threat hung in the air, a cold and terrible promise, and the first man fell silent, his body rigid with fear. The third man remained still, his gaze fixed on the approaching riders, his face unreadable. His fingers did not tremble, though they gripped the hilt of his blade with white intensity.

The hoofbeats grew louder, the sound reverberating through the forest like a heartbeat. Banquo's voice drifted toward them, calm and steady, a beacon of warmth in the cold, oppressive night. The murderers exchanged a final glance, their expressions taut with the weight of their unspoken doubts.

The second man nodded, his jaw set, and the others followed suit. The die was cast. There was no turning back now. As the riders drew near, the forest seemed to hold its breath, the wind stilling, the shadows deepening.

"Then we stand," muttered the first, though his words followed the third man's deeds.

The murderers stepped forward, their figures blending with the darkness, and the path ahead was swallowed by the night.

The riders approached the ambush, their horses' hooves muffled by the damp forest floor. The night cloaked them in shadow, but the murderers could make out the faint glint of Banquo's armour beneath his cloak and the pale, youthful face of Fleance beside him. Banquo spoke softly to his son, his voice steady, though the words did not carry beyond the rustling leaves.

"Give us a light there, ho!"

"That's him," one said, his tone tightening. "The others—the court guests—are all inside. This road's meant for no one else."

"He's taken the long way," said the youth. "As he does. Most men walk this mile from gate to hill. It helps the appetite before supper."

They saw the glow before the shapes: a torch held high, and beside it the broad silhouette of Banquo on horseback, his son riding close beside. The torch threw gold across wet leaves, and for a moment it looked as though the forest had taken fire at its core.

"A light," one of the murderers whispered. "A light."

The boy's voice rang out, young and unaware: "It smells of rain, father."

Banquo chuckled. "Aye—it will rain tonight."

"Let it come down!"

In a sudden burst of movement, the murderers leaped forward, blades flashing in the moonlight. The horses reared, their cries splitting the stillness as Banquo sprang from his saddle with the ease of a practiced warrior. Fleance cried out, clutching the reins as his horse danced wildly, but his father's voice cut through the chaos.

"O, treachery. Fly, good Fleance, run!" Banquo's command was urgent, unyielding.

The boy hesitated, his eyes wide with fear, but Banquo's shout pierced the night. "Now! Fly, fly, fly while you can and live! You may yet avenge this shadow of a man."

Fleance spurred his horse forward, its hooves pounding the earth as it bolted into the darkness. The third murderer made to follow, he movements lithe and quick, his blade raised with almost ceremonial precision, but Banquo was upon him in an instant, striking with the force of a man who had fought a thousand battles.

"Damn you—damn you all. O, slave—hell-sent, crawling bastard—"

The dagger was knocked from the murderer's grasp, and he stumbled back, his cry of pain swallowed by the forest.

The first and second murderers surged forward, their blades slashing at Banquo, who turned to meet them with the desperate ferocity of a cornered stag. He struck the second man with his elbow, sending him sprawling, but the third was back on his feet, quicker than the eye, his knife grazing Banquo's side. Blood blossomed beneath his cloak, dark and glistening, but still, he fought on.

"You'll not find cowards here," Banquo growled, his voice like thunder, his eyes blazing with defiance. He turned on the second murderer again, his movements sharp and precise, but the third came at him from behind, his blade plunging deep into Banquo's back.

The forest seemed to shudder with the force of the blow. Banquo staggered, his breath hitching as the strength drained from his limbs. The murderers closed in, their blades glinting as they struck again and again, until the great man fell to his knees, his blood pooling at their feet.

The first murderer stood frozen, his dagger hanging limp in his hand, his face pale as the moonlight that filtered through the trees. "This… this isn't right," he muttered, his voice shaking. "It wasn't supposed to be like this."

The second man, his face twisted with fury and bloodlust, turned on him. "He's dead. That's all that matters."

But Banquo was not yet gone. He lifted his head, his breath laboured, his eyes filled with a light that seemed to pierce the very souls of his attackers. Blood dripped from his lips as he spoke, his voice low but steady, carrying the weight of a curse.

"You may kill me," he rasped, his gaze locking on the second murderer. "But the throne will not be yours. Nor his."

The murderers exchanged uneasy glances, their confidence faltering beneath Banquo's words. The forest seemed to lean in, the shadows thickening, the air growing colder.

"My line will rise," Banquo continued, his voice stronger now, defiant even in the face of death. "Mark me, cowards. The blood of kings runs in my son's veins. You may try to snuff it out, but you will fail."

The third murderer hesitated, his blade trembling in his hand. "Enough of this," he muttered, stepping back as though to escape the power of Banquo's gaze.

The second murderer snarled, his rage boiling over. "Die, then," he spat, raising his blade for the final blow. But Banquo's laughter stopped him, low and bitter, like the rumble of distant thunder.

"You think this is the end?" Banquo said, his lips curving into a faint, bloodstained smile. "No. This is only the beginning."

With that, he slumped forward, his body still at last. The forest was silent, save for the laboured breathing of the murderers. The second man wiped his blade on his cloak, his movements jerky, as though trying to rid himself of the weight of Banquo's final words.

The first murderer stared at the lifeless body, his hands trembling. "The boy," he said suddenly, his voice breaking the heavy silence. "He escaped."

The second man's head snapped up, his eyes narrowing. "What?"

"The boy," the first repeated, gesturing toward the path where Fleance had vanished. "He's gone."

The third murderer cursed under his breath, his face darkening. "We were supposed to kill them both. That was the order." Yet he did not pursue.

The second man's grip tightened on his blade, his expression a storm of fury and fear. "We'll find him," he growled. "He can't have gone far."

But the first man shook his head, his voice trembling. "He's gone. And his father's words... they'll haunt us. You heard him. He cursed us."

The forest seemed to echo his words, the shadows closing in around them as the wind rose, carrying with it the faintest sound—a boy's cry, fading into the distance, a ghostly echo that lingered in their ears.

The second murderer spat on the ground, his face twisted with frustration. "Curses are for fools and cowards," he snarled. "We've done what we came to do. The rest is no concern of ours."

The third said nothing. His blade hung slack at his side, and for a moment, he looked not at Banquo, but down the path where the boy had vanished.

The two older men turned and disappeared into the darkness, leaving Banquo's body lying still among the trees, his blood staining the earth.

A faint breeze stirred the leaves, and the moon emerged once more, its pale light illuminating the path. The scene seemed frozen in time, the world holding its breath as though waiting for the consequences to unfold.

And somewhere, far beyond the reach of the murderers' blades, Fleance rode through the darkness, his heart pounding with fear and grief. His father's voice echoed in his mind, a command that rang with love and desperation: Fly, good Fleance, fly! He gripped the reins tightly, his young hands trembling, and urged the horse onward, the trees rushing past in a blur.

ACT III SCENE 4

The dining hall at Dunsinane Castle blazed with torchlight, the flames held high in great iron sconces that cast monstrous shadows across the tapestried walls. Long tables stretched the length of the chamber, adorned with silver trenchers, garlands of herbs, and flagons of wine that caught the firelight like pools of dark garnet.

The air was thick with the scent of roasted meats and tallow smoke. Beneath it all, something rank lingered—faint, but insistent—like damp wool, or the iron tang of a blade too recently wiped clean.

Macbeth entered first, resplendent in robes heavy with embroidery, but his steps bore the stiffness of a man rehearsing peace. He raised his arm, gesturing for the assembly to still.

"You know your places," he said, voice calm, though the firelight did strange things to his face. "Sit. From the highest to the lowest, you are all most heartily welcome."

The lords and thanes bowed slightly, murmuring in unison:

"Thanks to your majesty."

The sound carried like a tide, soft but calculated, the voice of men measuring their praise against their safety.

"We shall move among you," Macbeth continued, stepping from the dais and down into the space between the tables. "We're merely your host this night—not your king. Our gracious queen keeps her place above, but soon, I'll call upon her to lend her voice of welcome."

Lady Macbeth, already seated in her high-backed chair, offered a graceful nod. Her gown shimmered like oil on water, though her hands curled slightly in her lap.

"Say it for me then, sir," she said, smiling. "To all our friends. For my heart speaks truly—they are welcome."

Just then, the great door at the end of the hall creaked open—not loud, but enough to twist Macbeth's head like a hound catching scent. A boy had entered: a servant, no more than seventeen, clothes mud-streaked and dishevelled from travel. His face was unreadable, pale beneath a film of sweat, his hair dark with rain or something thicker.

He stood just inside the threshold, silent.

Macbeth crossed swiftly to him, intercepting him before the lords could notice the interruption. His hand fell on the boy's shoulder—not with warmth, but weight.

"There's blood on your face," he murmured.

The boy did not flinch.

"It's Banquo's," he said.

The words fell like stones into water.

"Better on your face," Macbeth replied, his voice now quieter still, "than in his veins."

His eyes bored into the boy's. "Is he dead?"

The servant nodded, once.

"I cut his throat. Myself."

Macbeth's lips parted in something like a smile—though it lacked joy, or triumph.

"Then you are the best of cut-throats. Unless you did the same for Fleance. Did you?"

The boy blinked. A pause.

"Fleance escaped."

It was not regret that coloured his tone. Not even fear. Just fact.

And Macbeth's face, so carefully sculpted moments before, fractured.

"Then my sickness returns," he said, almost to himself. "I would have been whole, strong as stone, untouchable as air... But now I'm caged—cramped—hemmed in by doubt and fear again."

He gripped the edge of the table nearest him, eyes flicking about the hall as though he might see the boy galloping back through the door.

"But Banquo... he's safe?"

The servant gave the smallest nod.

"Aye. Safe in a ditch. He lies with twenty gashes to his head. Any one of them would have ended him."

Macbeth exhaled sharply, as if releasing venom.

"Good. There lies the grown serpent. The worm that fled—he'll breed poison one day, but he has no fangs yet."

He waved his hand sharply.

"Go, Seyton. We'll speak again tomorrow."

The boy inclined his head once.

The young servant disappeared into the gloom, as if the shadows had swallowed him whole.

Macbeth turned back toward the feast, dragging a smile over his face like a man donning a mask made of wax. He climbed back to the dais, seating himself beside Lady Macbeth.

But she had seen it—the stiffness of his limbs, the paleness beneath his eyes.

"My royal lord," she whispered. "You've not shown your joy. This feast is not merely meat—it is ceremony. You must vouch your welcome, or all this," she gestured subtly to the gold and fire, "is but a marketplace."

Macbeth reached for his goblet and held it up, the red liquid trembling faintly.

"Sweet reminder," he said. "You always see what I forget."

He stood, holding the cup high.

"Let appetite meet good digestion," he declared. "And health to both."

The fire cracked sharply as Macbeth returned to his place at the table, lifting his cup again with a forced ease. He scanned the room with calculated charm, searching the shadows as if for reassurance, or perhaps a sign. He raised his voice just enough to command the room.

"Here we sit beneath the honour of our land's great names—were Banquo here, it would be complete."

He paused, letting the words breathe.

"But I'll take his absence as a discourtesy, not misfortune. Surely he has no ill fate—just a failing in manners."

There was a ripple of quiet laughter, the sound of men unsure how to respond.

"Indeed," said Ross, lifting his cup, "his absence does cast shadow on his promise. Will your highness grace the table with your company?"

Macbeth turned.

"The table's full."

Lennox, pointing gently, offered a place beside him.

"Here, my lord—there's space reserved."

And as Macbeth turned—

The seat where he had just stood—his own throne—was no longer empty.

A figure had taken it.

The shape of a man. Cloaked in shadow. His eyes—if they were eyes—locked on Macbeth's. There, seated in his place, sat Banquo.

Blood clung to the ghost's hair and dripped down his temple in slow, cold lines. His garments were torn, soaked through. He made no sound, no movement. Only his eyes met Macbeth's—and in them sat the quiet horror of truth returned from the earth.

"Who among you has done this?" Macbeth's voice cut sharp, the goblet trembling in his hand.

The lords turned, puzzled.

"What, my good lord?"

Macbeth pointed, his hand shaking.

"You can't accuse me—not me!" he cried, his eyes never leaving the phantom. "Don't shake your gory locks at me—I did not strike you!"

The ghost said nothing. His silence was more damning than words.

Chairs scraped back. Several men rose from their places, unease spreading like a spill of wine.

"Gentlemen," Ross said quickly, "the king is unwell."

Lady Macbeth stood in a smooth sweep of silk and shadow.

"Sit. Stay. He's often like this—since he was a child. It passes quickly." She smiled too brightly. "If you fuss, you'll only make it worse."

She swept across the dais and took her husband's arm, drawing him slightly aside.

"Are you a man?" she hissed, her voice barely above a whisper.

"Aye," Macbeth said, breathless, "a bold one. One who dares look on things that would turn the devil white."

Lady Macbeth's fingers dug into his sleeve.

"This is nonsense," she said. "Just fear dressed up as vision. It's like that dagger you claimed led you to Duncan's chamber. Fleeting, absurd—tales a child might tremble over at a winter fire, told by a grandmother for thrill. This isn't strength, it's shame."

Macbeth pulled slightly away from her grasp, his eyes wild.

"Look—there!" he said, pointing. "Do you see him? Look! What would it matter if he could speak? If graves give up the dead, and the tombs throw out their occupants, then what are monuments but meat for kites and crows?"

He stared again at the phantom, who still said nothing. Just sat, a presence where no presence should be.

And then—the ghost was gone.

One moment there; the next, the seat was empty, the blood vanished, the silence even deeper.

Lady Macbeth straightened.

"Have you lost all sense?"

Macbeth, still breathing heavily, turned toward her.

"I swear to you—standing here, I saw him."

She shook her head slowly, her lips tight.

"Fie, shame. Enough."

But Macbeth wasn't listening. His voice dropped to something low and bitter, as if speaking to himself—or to the hall itself.

"Blood has been spilled before," he said. "Before laws softened the world—men were murdered, and it was done. They died. That was the end."

His hands flexed against the table, the knuckles bone-white.

"Even now, there are murders done—acts too terrible to speak aloud. But back then, when the brain was smashed, the body stayed dead. It did not... sit at the table again."

He turned slowly back toward the vacant seat.

"But now they rise. With twenty wounds upon their crowns. And they drive the living from their seats."

Lady Macbeth moved closer, her voice steady but tight.

"My lord," she said softly. "Your noble guests lack your presence."

She glanced once toward the lords, who whispered uneasily, their fingers toying with goblets, glancing toward the doors, toward each other.

Far off, the wind moaned across the castle's stones.

Macbeth stood again, wiping his brow with a trembling hand, the tremor barely disguised behind his cup.

"Forgive me," he said to the room, his voice brittle but regal. "My friends, do not be startled. I suffer from a strange condition—nothing, truly, to those who know me. It passes."

He managed a smile—thin, cracked.

"To your healths. Love and health to all. And now... I'll sit. Pour me wine—fill it to the brim."

A servant stepped forward and filled Macbeth's cup without a word, and withdrew like a scared boy after being dared to goad a tiger.

Macbeth lifted the goblet.

"I drink to the joy of this table, and to our absent friend Banquo." He paused. "Whom we miss." His voice caught briefly, then steadied. "Would that he were here. To Banquo—and to all!"

"Our duties, and the pledge," murmured the lords, raising their cups, not knowing what devils clung to the stem their king's cup.

The goblets clinked softly.

Then the world tilted.

It did not shatter, not yet. It tilted—just enough that the wine slipped sideways in the goblets, and the hearth's fire seemed to breathe backward. Someone laughed, or coughed, or maybe wept—but the sound bent like heat, stretched thin and wrong.

Macbeth turned to sit—

—and Banquo was not in the chair.

He was everywhere.

He stood by the hearth. No—no, he was in the wall. No—he was behind Macbeth's eyes, pressing against them like the soft skin of fruit gone rotten. His outline flickered with flame-light, shifting between a man and a sculpture of blood, wearing a crown of wounds. The wounds smiled where his mouth did not.

Macbeth stumbled backward, the floor beneath him no longer stone, but something breathing, rippling like muscle.

"Avaunt!" His voice rang across the hall. Conversation halted, and forks were lowered in mid-air.

"Get from me! Let the earth hide you, bury you again!"

But Banquo did not move. His limbs remained stiff, dead, but his head turned slowly, like a door closing. His eyes—those horrible, unmoving eyes—held no light, no thought, and yet Macbeth saw himself reflected in them, standing in the throne room with Duncan's blood on his hands, laughing before it dried.

"You have no marrow in your bones," Macbeth hissed, pointing. "Your blood runs cold. Your eyes—they see nothing, and yet you stare as though you see everything."

Macbeth said, and the words were not his—they were the forest speaking, the stone, the scream of sleep that would not come.

The fire surged. The feast dissolved. The lords and thanes were gone. The whole of Dunsinane peeled away like flesh from bone.

Macbeth was no longer at the banquet. He was on the moors, he would have welcomed even the witches' presence, he felt so utterly alone.

He stood in a place where nothing cast a shadow, and Banquo was the only figure that remained—huge, towering, his form stitched from the sins Macbeth had dared not name aloud. Around him, Duncan knelt, smiling at the throat, Fleance ran eternally into woods without end, and Lady Macbeth wept in a weaning chamber that did not exist.

"What man dares," Macbeth cried, staggering forward, "I dare!"

"Come at me in the form of beasts! A bear! A rhinoceros! A tiger with teeth made of iron! I will not flinch!"

He turned, looking for a sword, for his own hands—but he had no body now, only the howl of guilt and the fire behind his eyes.

"Take any shape but this one," he whispered now, tears bleeding from the corners of his soul. "Just not that. Don't come as you are, Banquo. Come as storm, as plague, as famine, but not as you."

His voice cracked. The walls reassembled around him—too fast, too loud.

"Back to your grave!" he shrieked. "Back to the dark!"

And Banquo vanished.

Just like that.

He was gone.

The table returned. The goblet still lay in Macbeth's hand. The fire was tame again. The lords stared. Lady Macbeth stood like marble—her eyes burning beneath her crown.

"He's gone," Macbeth muttered. "So... I am a man again. Sit. Sit, please."

Silence stretched long and terrible.

Lady Macbeth's voice cracked through it like a whip made of silver.

Lady Macbeth's voice was tight with fury, though her smile remained pinned like a brooch.

"You've killed the mood. Broken the company. Turned merriment into a spectacle."

Macbeth looked over the room, the wary eyes watching him like so many wolves in human skin.

"Do such things just happen?" he asked aloud. "Like clouds that pass in summer—sudden, strange, and gone again? Am I the only one amazed? You all seem so calm—so flushed with good cheer—while I go pale with fear."

Ross leaned forward, tentative.

"What sights, my lord?"

But Lady Macbeth's hand snapped out like a whip.

"Do not press him," she said, her voice cold. "It makes him worse. Speak no more. The night is done."

She turned back to the guests, voice lifting.

"Good night, my lords. Stand not on ceremony. Go at once."

The hall emptied. Quietly. Relieved. As if departing a chamber of plague. The guests rose, shuffling with confusion and careful restraint. Some offered murmurs of sympathy, others only bows. Lennox, pale-faced and tight-lipped, offered a final word:

"Good night. May better health attend the king."

Lady Macbeth bowed her head slightly.

"A kind good night to all."

The doors closed behind them. The hall was empty, save for the two of them. The torches flickered lower. Seyton remained in the far shadows, still and unseen.

Macbeth turned from the table, his voice low and bitter.

"It will have blood, they say—blood will have blood. Stones have been known to speak. Trees have whispered. The wind carried secrets to birds, who told men of murders best buried. There are signs in the earth. Insects have betrayed their masters."

Lady Macbeth's voice had lost its edge, now soft and distant.

"It's near morning. The sky cannot decide whether it's night or dawn."

Macbeth nodded, slowly.

"And Macduff... he refused our summons."

She tensed.

"Did you send for him?"

"No," Macbeth said, "but I heard it whispered. I'll send now. I've placed spies in every house—men on my coin, watching. But tomorrow—tomorrow I go to the witches."

He stared into the fire.

"They know more. I'll force it from them if I must. I need certainty—even if it ruins me. From now on, anything that stands in my way must fall."

He turned to her fully now.

"I'm already drenched in blood. If I stopped here, turning back would be as long as pressing on. There are things in my mind that must find action, or they'll rot in place."

Lady Macbeth reached out to him.

"You need rest. The one thing all living things require—sleep."

But he only nodded.

"Yes. Sleep. Let's go. What I feel is fear, but it needs practice. We are... still young in wickedness."

They walked from the hall, the shadows stretching behind them like long black spears.

ACT III SCENE 5

Gathered in silence, the witches occupied a blasted hollow marked by twisted yew and scorched stone. The night was thick as congealed breath, the moor swaddled in fog that moved like the skirts of unseen dancers. Hollow crags jutted from the earth like broken teeth. At their centre, the witches' fire hissed without flame, fed by roots and whispers. The First Witch crouched over the embers, grinding dried wolf's bane between her fingers. A wind cut across the moor, cold and sharp, carrying something else within its keen. The air turned heavy, tasting of iron. She looked up from her bone-piled circle, her split lips curling faintly as she squinted into the swirling gloom. "How now, Hecate?" she croaked. "You wear your anger like thunder."

And then she came. Hecate descended not like a woman, but like a comet trailing a curse—her shape streaming through the sky, ribbons of ice and shadow flowing behind her like tattered crow's wings. The ground seemed to shudder beneath her footfall. The fire coiled low to her hem, guttering as if afraid. Her face was young and ancient, and her eyes shone with cold authority, glowing like coins lost in the well of the world.

Her voice struck the stone like thunder wrapped in silk.

Have I not cause, you hags so bold,
To curse your deeds, both rash and cold?

The witches shrank under her voice, stiffening as even the fire dared not crackle.

How dared you meddle with Macbeth—
In riddles dark and songs of death—
While I, who lead your sacred art,
The mother of all spells that start,
Was never called to lend my skill,
Nor bade to shape the fated will?

She stepped into the circle, and the flames retreated further. The First Witch lowered her head, unable to meet that burning gaze. Hecate's voice dropped, low and deadly.

And worse: your work, though sly and slyer,
Was spent upon a wayward squire—
A wrathful man, consumed with pride,
Who loves for gain, with none beside.

A silence fell, thick and listening. The witches trembled, the wind moaning as though the moor itself regretted hearing her words. But then Hecate lifted her chin, her expression shifting.

But make it right—depart with speed,
To Acheron, where shadows feed.
At break of day, meet me there soon,

Beneath the pit and hanging moon.
He comes to seek what fate has spun;
Prepare your spells, leave naught undone.

The witches began to stir, gathering their vials and talismans, their movements quick and nervous under her command. Hecate turned, her cloak unfurling like smoke released from bone.

I take to air—this night I chase
A doom to shake both time and place.
Ere noon strikes high, our work must bloom;
A drop now hangs upon the moon,
A misty pearl of magic deep—
I'll snatch it ere it dares to weep.
Distilled through rites the dark approves,
It shall raise phantoms none can move.
Their haunting shapes, through false delight,
Will draw him deeper into night.
He'll scorn at fate, and mock the dead,
His hopes puffed high, his wisdom fled.
She turned back to them, her gaze like a blade.
And you all know—how fair it seems—
False safety is the death of dreams.

Just then, a sound pierced the night: eerie, thin, and high—like a reed flute played underwater. It came from nowhere and everywhere at once. Hecate smiled, her teeth white as frost.

"Hark—do you hear?" she murmured, pointing towards the edge of the circle where a grey cloud hovered, shifting and waiting. "My little spirit calls. He sits in fog and waits beyond the walls. My chariot waits the turn."

With that, she raised one arm and vanished in a crackle of smoke and ozone. The stones where she had stood steamed faintly. The fire extinguished completely, plunging the hollow into deeper shadow.

The witches were silent for a breath, the air still ringing with power. The First Witch blinked into the space where Hecate had stood, the lingering scent of storm in the air.

"Come," she said, her voice hoarse with awe and urgency. "Let's make haste. She'll not be long."

And with a hiss of skirts and the rustle of unseen wings lifting from the darkened trees, the witches were gone, their footprints scorched into the moss like brands. The heath fell silent once more—except for the moon, caught weeping its single, trembling drop above the place where fate would soon be undone.

ACT III SCENE 6

Beneath the vaults of Elgin's early church—neither fully cathedral nor mere chapel—two figures moved in careful proximity. One, Lord Lennox, cloaked in fur against the Highland chill, paced slowly, his boots soft against the worn flagstones. The other, robed in ecclesiastical garb of deep claret, stood by an iron candelabrum where wax had wept upon the floor in layers like fallen petals. This man had no name on the lips of nobles, but his letters bore the mark of Dunkeld's authority, and no one in Moray questioned whom he served. The cloister's arches curved like the ribs of some great stone beast, ribbed and ancient, whispering the secrets of centuries. Between them hung a breathless hush, broken only by the sigh of the wind through narrow windows and the restless creak of a wooden door left half ajar. The northern sky beyond was purpled and heavy with mist, the cold coming in like water into an untended boat.

Lennox folded his hands behind his back, glancing briefly at a carved relief of the Passion above the cloister's inner door. "My words must not outpace your thoughts," he said at last, voice hushed. "But surely you see the shape of things. A pattern that repeats itself beneath the guise of accident."

The robed figure, his face part-shadowed by the candlelight, did not immediately reply. He was polishing the ring upon his index finger.

Lennox pressed on, his tone tighter, sharp with the need to speak where court had grown silent. "Duncan, so grievously mourned—after he was dead. Banquo, cut down in the dark of night—by Fleance, they say. Though what child, grieving his father's murder, flees without denial?"

He paused. The old priest said nothing, but his dark eyes flicked to meet Lennox's, the faintest gleam of something knowing—amused, even—sparking there.

Lennox's voice dropped further. "Aye. Men must not walk late, or they will find themselves buried early."

He turned from the stone wall, drawing his cloak tighter. "And Malcolm and Donalbain—how monstrous their guilt must be, to flee so quickly. Did it not pierce the good Macbeth's heart? That in pious rage he slew their guards before they could speak a word?"

At this, the priest gave a low sound—half breath, half scoff. Whether it was approval or dismissal was impossible to tell. He reached for a flask of iron-hued wine and poured two cups, offering one to Lennox.

"Drink," he said softly. "It is cold this far north. And colder yet in the king's regard."

Lennox accepted, but did not sip. "Aye, he has borne all things well. So nobly, so wisely. Were Duncan's sons in his keeping, I daresay he would show them what comes of slaying a father." His voice was bitter now, the taste of iron not from wine but memory. "As he would Fleance—should the boy be found."

He stepped to the cloister's edge, gazing out through the stone lattice at the fog-shrouded graveyard beyond. "Macduff, I hear, is in disgrace. Gone from the feast without a word. Do you know where he has gone?"

The priest placed his cup down gently. "To England," he said, as if discussing the weather. "To the court of King Edward."

Lennox turned, startled. "And is Malcolm still there?"

"He is. The Confessor receives him with the honour due a prince dispossessed," said the old priest, his voice calm, his hands folded again within his sleeves. "No storm of fortune can tarnish the grace Edward shows. There Macduff seeks counsel, and not counsel only."

Lennox narrowed his gaze. "He calls on Northumberland?"

The priest inclined his head slightly. "Siward is a man not easily stirred, but for Malcolm and the good of Scotland, he may be roused."

A silence stretched between them then. From the high beams above, a small scattering of dust drifted down, catching the candlelight like ash.

The priest continued, his tone low and reverent, as if offering a prayer: "Should Heaven itself choose to ratify the work, we may yet see peace return to our tables, and knives removed from our feasts. Sleep for our nights. Honour for our oaths. All that now lies broken beneath blood and silence."

Lennox drew a slow breath. "And Macbeth? What does he?"

The priest's expression sharpened, just a touch. "He prepares," he said. "Not for penance."

"Sent he to Macduff?" Lennox asked.

A small smile played on the older man's lips—humourless, dry. "He did. But Macduff sent word back with a 'Sir, not I,' and the messenger's face darkened with it. He hummed like a man who knows his note shall be remembered."

The wind pushed at the cloister's ancient wood, and for a moment, the candle flame fluttered and bent low.

Lennox turned toward the altar steps, but did not kneel. "Then Macduff must guard his distance. May some holy angel fly to England and warn them of what comes. May Heaven's blessing outrun the tyrant's shadow."

He bowed his head, more in weariness than faith. "Let this land not suffer much longer beneath a hand accursed."

The old priest stepped closer then, his hand lifting—not to bless, but to steady. He placed it briefly on Lennox's shoulder, heavy with meaning. "God's blessing go with him," he said, voice barely more than breath. "And with those who make good of bad, and friends of foes."

And then he turned, his robes whispering against the stone as he moved through the cloister. From some hidden corridor, his guards emerged and fell into step behind him. Their boots made no more sound than the passing of time. Lennox remained alone beneath the crucifix and the carvings of the saints, feeling the cold settle into his bones—and wondering how long prayers could hold the storm at bay.

ACT IV

ACT IV SCENE 1

As Macbeth rode deeper into the forest the air grew colder, the pale light of the moon casting jagged shadows across the gnarled trees. The woods were ancient, their roots clawing at the earth as though trying to escape the taint of the place. A heavy mist clung to the ground, swirling around the hooves of the horses and muffling their steps.

Behind Macbeth rode Lennox and a small retinue of mounted men — cloaked figures hunched against the wind, eyes wary, their torches low and sputtering. They spoke little, and only in hushed tones. Even the horses seemed to sense that this place was wrong.

The wind whispered through the branches, its voice soft and mournful, carrying words no man could quite make out.

Macbeth halted at a bend in the path where the trees gave way to open stone. Before them loomed a jagged outcropping of moorstone, black as oil, rising from the earth like a broken tooth. A narrow cleft yawned beneath it — the entrance to the cavern.

He turned in his saddle, his voice clipped but firm.

"Wait here. None of you are to follow."

Lennox frowned but said nothing. Rain pattered on his shoulders as he dismounted, brushing water from his brow.

"My lord," he said quietly, "shall I not at least—"

"No."

Macbeth's tone held no room for discussion. "This is not a place for men."

A long silence. Then a nod.

Macbeth dismounted and moved alone toward the cavern mouth, his cloak streaming behind him, the mist swallowing him in moments.

His face was a mask of determination, though his eyes betrayed the turmoil within.

Thunder cracked like the wrath of a sky torn asunder, its sound reverberating through the bones of the hills. The cavern lay deep within the earth, secreted beneath a jagged shelf of moorstone that jutted like a broken tooth from the wilderness. Rain hissed through the fissures above, snaking down the slick rock walls to weep upon the black-stained floor. Here, beneath Scotland's skin, the three women gathered once more.

The fire at the centre of the chamber was old and ancient in its spirit, fed not by wood alone but by herbs that stank of rot and bitterness. The cauldron that squatted atop it was not forged by any honest blacksmith. Its iron seemed to sweat, to pulse, to breathe — a container for the vortex of a nightmare.

The first of the witches — crooked-backed and weather-laced, her flesh the hue of ash after storm — tilted her head sharply, as if some inaudible summons had pierced her mind. Her tongue flicked across cracked lips before she rasped, "Thrice the brinded cat hath mewed." The words sounded like wind scouring a crypt — dry, brittle, echoing with something old and unkind.

"Thrice and once the hedge-pig whined," intoned the second, her voice higher, cloying, as though sweetened with poison. Her face bore the cunning of small creatures — rats in the rafters, foxes at the edge of torchlight — and her hands were always moving, twitching, clawing at the air as if plucking thoughts from invisible threads.

From the gloom near the wall, the third stepped forward, taller than the others and silent until now. Her hair hung in lank ropes, wet with cave-damp, and her eyes glistened with unspoken hunger. "Harpier cries: 'Tis time, 'tis time."

The cauldron answered her with a low burble, releasing a plume of yellowed steam that smelled of bile and rust. A toad was drawn from the folds of the first witch's cloak — its belly grey and slick with death. She tossed it in with a sound like spit hitting coals. "Toad, that under cold stone hath lain a month and one; swelter'd venom, sleeping got — boil thou first in the charmed pot."

The three leaned in, their voices coiling together, rising in rhythm, a litany woven with salt and malice:
"Double, double, toil and trouble;
Fire burn and cauldron bubble."
The chant did not simply echo in the cavern — it lived there, rattling the very bones of the stone, seeping into every crack and whispering to the earth beyond.

"Fillet of a fenny snake," crooned the second, her arms pale as moonlight as she plunged them into a sack. She drew forth the serpentine flesh, slick and coiling in death's last twitch. "In the cauldron boil and bake."

"Eye of newt and toe of frog," she continued, dropping them in one by one, the liquids hissing in reply. "Wool of bat and tongue of dog. Adder's fork and blind-worm's sting, lizard's leg and owlet's wing." The pieces slapped and hissed, an orchestra of suffering. "For a charm of powerful trouble — like a hell-broth, boil and bubble!"

Again, the chorus rose — shrill, rhythmic, ceremonial:

"Double, double, toil and trouble;
Fire burn and cauldron bubble."

The third witch stepped forward now, with something wrapped in an oil-soaked rag. As she unwrapped it, the stench filled the air: scale of dragon, tooth of wolf, witches' mummy — ground down bone dust of those who whispered prophecy in their madness. "Maw and gulf of the ravined salt-sea shark," she said, eyes wide with ecstasy. "Root of hemlock digged in the dark, liver of blaspheming Jew—"

"Gall of goat and slips of yew," added the first, "slivered in the moon's eclipse. Nose of Turk and Tartar's lips, finger of birth-strangled babe ditch-delivered by a drab."

The last item was a wrinkled, purpling thing — a relic of cruelty — and it slipped from her fingers with reverence into the frothing vat. The potion swelled, thick and bubbling like a swamp digesting its prey. "Make the gruel thick and slab," she whispered. "Add thereto a tiger's chaudron — for the ingredients of our cauldron!"

The three joined again in their refrain, this time louder, their voices growing frantic as the air shimmered with unseen energy:

"Double, double, toil and trouble;

Fire burn and cauldron bubble."

The second witch brought forth a small vessel, its contents hidden, sealed with red wax and braided hair. "Cool it with a baboon's blood," she said, voice shaking with awe, "then the charm is firm and good."

Just then, the wind changed. It did not blow, but entered. A pressure swelled inside the cavern, not from any direction but from within the bones of the air itself. The flame bent low, not in fear, but as if forced to kneel. The rocks shivered in place, the iron tang of the cauldron thickened, clotted with something older, something unclean and infinite.

She was here.

Not in form, but an invasion of the mind, not a shape, but as a change in reality itself.

The darkness at the edges of the chamber bled. Shadows turned inward like peeling flesh, folding space in a way that made the walls seem both inches and miles apart. And within that torn veil of vision, there emerged a knowing god in woman's form. Hecate — unbounded by body, pressing into the minds of the witches like a fever dream they could not wake from.

She wore no face — or perhaps she wore all of them, flickering like reflections on black water. Her awareness filled their lungs, their skulls, the marrow of their bones, and the words she spoke were not heard but experienced — too loud and too soft at once, like thunder whispered into the soul.

"Well done," Her voice moved like silk soaked in oil, catching on thorns, parting like flesh. It echoed not across the chamber but across the veins of the witches, down the ridges of their spines.

"I commend your pains.

And every one shall share in the gains."

The witches twitched in synchrony, their mouths slack, eyes rolling white. Her presence wrapped around them like a wet cloth — oppressive, intimate, inescapable. Her words were not command but compulsion:

"Now about the cauldron sing,
Like elves and fairies in a ring,
Enchanting all that you put in."

And so they moved, though they did not remember choosing to. The rhythm infected their limbs — jerky at first, like puppets whose strings were wet, and then smoother, like wind through tall grass, unnatural and endless. A tune rose around them, not carried by any voice but exhaled by the cavern itself, a droning hymn that flattened time and space.

It was not music. It was a sound that remembered music.

The witches circled the fire, and as they chanted, their voices slurred and slithered into tones that bore no root in any tongue known to humankind. They were syllables birthed in unconscious places, behind the eyes, beneath language, where dreams gestate and rot. Their hands fluttered, reaching not toward the cauldron but toward invisible things that now breathed beside them — unseen but close, too close.

Hecate watched — or was the watching itself — her presence stretching through every dancing limb, every trembling joint. She was hunger and euphoria, blade and balm, mother and mutilator.

And then she was gone.

Not with sound. Not with light. Only with the sudden, staggering absence of her weight. Like waking from the brink of drowning — not rescued, merely released.

The silence that followed Hecate's withdrawal was not relief, but a wound — raw and ringing. The witches did not speak. They merely breathed, their mouths still shaped around the syllables they had conjured, the ghost of the chant staining their lips like bruises. They swayed where they stood, caught between trance and madness, the circle unbroken.

And then, a shift.

The second witch stilled — just for a moment — her fingers brushing her lips, her eyes rolling white as if touched by some gust of unseen knowledge.

"By the pricking of my thumbs," she murmured, her voice fraying at the edges, "something wicked this way comes."

She tilted her head toward the jagged entrance, where the storm clawed and howled. Her smile curled with cruel recognition.

"Open, locks — whoever knocks."

But she did not turn. None of them did. They kept dancing — slowly now, a weaving that seemed to glide just above the stone, their feet never quite touching. The fire hissed, the cauldron burbled thick and red, and the air pressed inward as if dreading what came next.

From beyond the veil of wind and stone, footsteps sounded — heavy, deliberate. The tread of a man who had gone too far and could no longer tell power from curse, prophecy from prison.

Macbeth came.

Broad-shouldered and hollow-eyed, his face scoured by sleepless nights and visions that clung like cobwebs to the corners of his gaze.

The scorpion amulet at his neck pulsed faintly, a dull red light as though something beneath his skin remembered pain.

He stepped through the mouth of the cavern, the world narrowing around him — framed by oozing stone and the snap of eldritch flame. The very air recoiled from him, and still the witches danced, unbroken, unwelcoming.

The rain that clung to his cloak did not glisten — it wept from him, as though the elements themselves sought to flee. Each drop slid from his shoulders, rejected.

His voice cracked the moment like a blade striking old bone:

"How now, you secret, black, and midnight hags."

It was not greeting, nor accusation — but something twisted between the two. His tone, once noble, now bore the weight of exhaustion and a bitter kind of awe. He looked on them not with fear, but with loathing, and just enough reverence to make that loathing dangerous.

The witches did not answer. They only turned — mid-step — and their eyes fixed on him without stilling their motion. Their mouths twitched into faint, knowing smiles, like crows watching a lamb twist in the snow.

Macbeth's voice dropped, rough with disdain:

"What is it you do?" the smell of the cauldron turned his stomach, his hunger replaced with the hope that he would not be expected to drink of that foul broth.

They stopped all at once, and each one turned at the same time to pin him with their vision. Their reply was whispered, unified, and terrible:

"A deed without a name."

A tremor passed through him, almost imperceptible, as though the words struck not his ears but the roots of his soul. Yet he pressed on — for a man who has spilled the blood of kings must also kneel before demons if it serves his purpose.

"I conjure you," he said, stepping closer, his breath rising like steam in the witch-light. "By that which you profess—however you come to know it—answer me."

His voice rose — louder, harder — not with panic, but with the sheer force of desperation sharpened into command. Each word struck like a hammer against the vault of heaven.

"Even if you unleash the storm-winds and set them tearing through the churches...
Even if the oceans rise, foaming and wild, and swallow every ship that dares cross them...
Even if the wheat falls flat and the trees are ripped from the earth...
If castles collapse on the heads of their defenders, if palaces and temples crumble into their own foundations...
If all the seeds of nature — every last beginning — fall and rot before they bloom…
Even if the world itself turns sick from destruction — still you must answer me."
He stood trembling from the effort of holding himself back from the brink of something worse than rage.

The fire hissed. The air pulsed.

And then — not in chorus, but with eerie synchronicity — the witches replied.

"Speak," murmured the first, her eye glinting like coals turned inward.

"Demand," sighed the second, her fingers coiling as if plucking threads from the air.

"We'll answer," said the third, her grin thin and cold as a blade.

Each voice was distinct — yet together they struck like the notes of a single, discordant chord. Three voices. One will.

"Say," said the first, "would'st you hear it from our mouths, or from our master's?"

Macbeth did not hesitate. His voice was a clenched fist:

"Call 'em. Let me see 'em."

The witches' faces turned as if to some unseen herald. One plucked a handful of thick, curdled blood from a clay pot; another cradled fat scraped from the neck of a traitor swaying in the gallows wind. With ritualistic slowness, they fed these offerings to the fire.

"Pour in sow's blood, that hath eaten her nine farrow," crooned one, reverently.
"Grease that's sweaten from the murderer's gibbet—throw into the flame!"
The chant began again — but softer this time, not with the rhythm of incantation, but invocation:

"Come, high or low;
Thyself and office deftly show."
The thunder responded like a command obeyed. Macbeth stared, transfixed at the roiling landscape within the cauldron. It became the moors almost, he was trapped inside of it somehow. The fire surged, blue-white, and in its heart rose the First Apparition: a severed head,

crowned not with laurel nor gold but with iron twisted like the ribs of a burnt cathedral. Its eyes glowed, but not from within — something else moved inside the sockets, shifting wetly in the red light.

And there — coiled in the left hollow — a black scorpion, its tail curled protectively across the crown like a second diadem.

King Duncan. Or what was left of him. His beard still singed from torchlight, his mouth barely moving. Yet when he spoke, the voice came like gravel poured over a tombstone — distant, echoing with ancient war drums and coronation bells long extinguished.

Macbeth recoiled only slightly, his voice strained:

"Tell me, thou unknown power—"

The First Witch raised a hand, thin as smoke, silencing him.

"He knows thy thought. Hear his speech — but speak thou nought."

The crowned head twitched, and the scorpion shifted.

"Macbeth. Macbeth. Macbeth," it rasped.
"Beware Macduff.
Beware the Thane of Fife.
Dismiss me: enough."
And then it was gone — the iron crown crumbling into ash as the head fell back into the cauldron, leaving behind only a curl of black smoke that rose like a question no one dared answer.

Macbeth stepped forward, heart thundering in his throat.

"Whatever thou art, for thy good caution, thanks.
Thou hast harped my fear aright. But one word more—"
But the witches had already turned back to the fire, their hands outstretched.

The thunder cracked again — hotter, hungrier, splitting the very roof of the cavern with its sound. The cauldron was not full of liquid now, but fire. A blazing bonfire, shaped like a hall. From the flames emerged a figure swaddled in smoke and charred cloth. Flesh blistered and peeling, veins glowing with the last embers of a long-dead pyre. A man burned alive, and yet alive again — Gille Coemgáin, Macbeth's cousin and former Mormaer of Moray, until his murder left the seat for Macbeth to take, and from whom he had secured both wife and child. Gille's eyes — when they opened — were red pits of betrayal and something else: the hollow grief of a life rewritten.

"He will not be commanded," murmured the First Witch, her voice dreamy and detached. "Here's another, more potent than the first."

The apparition smiled — lips cracked, leaking soot.

"Macbeth. Macbeth. Macbeth."

Macbeth's mouth twitched. He tried sarcasm to fend off terror.

"Had I three ears, I'd hear thee."

The scorched man did not blink. He did not burn — he smouldered.

"Be bloody, bold, and resolute.
Laugh to scorn the power of man.
For none of woman born shall harm Macbeth."

The flames surged around him, and in a hiss of steam and ash, he vanished — leaving behind the stench of burnt meat and a single falling tooth, blackened and cracked.

Macbeth laughed — short, sharp, bitter.

"Then live, Macduff: what need I fear of thee?
But yet I'll make assurance double sure,

181

And take a bond of fate — thou shalt not live."

His gaze was wild now, glittering. A fever-dream laced his words.

"That I may tell pale-hearted fear it lies, and sleep — in spite of thunder."

A third clap shattered the air — and this time the fire did not part but bent, as though bowing to something sacred and terrible.

Through the flame stepped a child.

He was pale as moonstone, but crowned — a strange and lovely thing, dressed in silver leaves, with a branch of living green clasped in both hands. His face was too calm, his gaze too old. His crown was woven of yew and rowan, and in his pupils was the mirror of a thousand years. He looked not born but summoned.

And to those who knew — to witches and kings alike — his face was uncanny. It echoed a future king yet to come, child of prophecy, ghost of legacy, monarch carved from myth.

Macbeth's voice cracked.

"What is this…
That rises like the issue of a king,
And wears upon his baby-brow the round
And top of sovereignty?"
The witches whispered in eerie unison:

"Listen — but speak not to't."

The child lifted the branch — and the leaves shivered, though no wind touched them.

His voice was quiet. Certain.

"Be lion-mettled, proud. Take no care
Who chafes, who frets, or where conspirers are.
Macbeth shall never vanquished be, until
Great Birnam Wood to high Dunsinane Hill
Shall come against him."

And then he was gone — simply gone — as though time had folded over him and erased him from its page.

Macbeth staggered back, exhaling as though stabbed.

"That will never be. Who can impress the forest? Bid the tree
Unfix his earth-bound root? Sweet bodements — good."

He laughed again, softly this time. Not from joy.

"Let the rebellious dead lie still — until the forest of Birnam climbs to Dunsinane.

Until that day, Macbeth shall live out his days as fate allows."

But even as he spoke, his breath turned cold.

"Yet... my heart throbs to know one thing. Tell me, if your art
can tell so much —
Shall Banquo's issue ever reign in this kingdom?"
For the first time, the witches turned their eyes away from him.

Their voices were low. Final.

"Seek to know no more."

But Macbeth's fury rose, unrelenting.

"I will be satisfied! Deny me this,
And an eternal curse fall on you. Let me know!"

The cauldron hissed — blackened, blistering. The witches began to chant.

"Show!" cried the First.
"Show!" sang the Second.
"Show his eyes — and grieve his heart," intoned the Third.
"Come like shadows — so depart."
And from the smoke and fire came the pageant.

One by one, kings emerged, ghostly and crowned — each bearing the face of Banquo. Their features were strange combinations, flickering like candlelight in wind. Eyes full of judgment, brows circled in gold.

Macbeth staggered.

"Thou art too like the spirit of Banquo — down!"

Another.

"Thy crown does sear mine eye-balls."

And still another.

"And thy hair — thou other gold-bound brow — is like the first…"

The line seemed never-ending. A procession of power, stretching to the crack of doom.

"What, will the line stretch out to the crack of doom? Another yet. A seventh. I'll see no more."

And then, from behind the seventh king, a voice not of flesh but of heaven, not of the witches but older than prophecy itself — echoed across the chamber like thunder in a cathedral:

"The Son of man goeth as it is written of him:
but woe unto that man by whom the Son of man is betrayed!

It had been good for that man if he had not been born."

Macbeth froze. The words sank deeper than any blade. They did not belong to the witches. They were not conjured — they were scripture. And in them, he heard the sound of judgment.

Then the eighth king appeared, bearing the mirror — and the rest unfolded like divine indictment. The eighth held a mirror, and within its cold silver, Macbeth saw legions: kings unborn, sceptres raised, and a world that did not remember him. An in the mirror-vision, at the end — Banquo. His ghost stood bloodied, smiling with a mouth full of silence.

Macbeth let out a strangled sound, almost a sob, almost a curse.

"Horrible sight! Now I see 'tis true.
For the blood-boltered Banquo smiles upon me,
And points at them — for his."
The apparitions dissolved into time. And Macbeth was alone.

His heart beat ragged in his chest. His mouth tasted of iron. The witches watched him as a nursemaid watches a fevered child — not with care, but curiosity.

Finally, they broke the pregnant silence.

"Ay, sir," the First said gently. "All this is so. But why stands Macbeth thus amazedly?"

Their voices grew fainter as they began to dance — a strange, joyous, hideous thing — the music rising from no instrument, no hand, no world. The cavern itself pulsed with their movement, until, one by one, they vanished — into shadow, into wind, into nothing.

Hecate's laughter lingered behind.

The chamber seemed colder now. The air, which moments before had been thick with brimstone and flame, now hung hollow, disturbed only by the dying echoes of prophecy and the scorched scent of vanished spirits. The cauldron had collapsed inward on itself — a blackened husk — as though it had never held fire at all, only memory.

Macbeth stood motionless. His cloak was damp with sweat, though no heat remained. He blinked once, slow and vacant, as if returning from some place far beyond the mortal veil. His voice broke the silence, bitter and rasping:

"Where are they? Gone?"

He turned toward the empty space, searching shadows for the edges of their skirts, the remnants of laughter, but nothing remained. Only stone, only silence.

"Let this pernicious hour," he spat, "be branded into the bones of time, damned in every calendar."

His words curled like smoke in the air, clinging to the dark stone. There was no echo. The room itself seemed reluctant to carry the curse.

A sound stirred beyond the cavern's mouth — not a knock, but the scrape of boots against wet stone, the muted shuffle of someone reluctant to approach. The wind moaned through the narrow passageway, dragging with it the scent of rain and horse sweat.

"Well? Step inside. If you've come this far, then enter."

From the shadows beyond the flame's reach emerged Lennox, stiff-backed and pale, his face lined with tension. He stepped across the slick stone floor with the caution of a man who walks too near a starving wolf.

"What's your grace's will?" he asked, his voice careful, his eyes shifting too often for comfort.

Macbeth's gaze snapped toward him, searching his face for truth.

"Saw you the weird sisters?"

Lennox stiffened. "No, my lord," he said quickly, too quickly. He looked past Macbeth, to the blackened remnants of the fire, the scorched stone, the smear of something on the wall that did not look like soot.

He did not ask what had happened.

He did not want to know.

"Came they not by you?"

"No indeed, my lord."

A flicker passed through Macbeth's eyes — doubt, fury, resignation. He turned from Lennox with a snarl.

"Infected be the air they ride, and damned all those that trust them."

Lennox's breath caught slightly, his lips parting as though to respond — but he said nothing. He glanced toward the foul remains of ash and bone on the floor, and the tremble in his hands betrayed what his mouth would not.

"I did hear," Macbeth continued, his voice laced with tension, "the galloping of horse. Who was't came by?"

Lennox cleared his throat. "'Tis two or three, my lord," he said, eyes darting toward the darkened corridor. "They bring you word: Macduff is fled to England."

For a moment, Macbeth said nothing. The silence between them stretched until it strained.

"Fled to England," he repeated, quietly. Not a question, but a seal placed upon a death sentence.

"Ay, my good lord."

The title — my good lord — fell like a leaf into fire, curling at the edges. Lennox's gaze flicked toward the floor again. There was no exit in his voice, no rescue in his posture. He was a man surrounded by glass and iron — shattering with every breath, yet trapped within the frame of loyalty.

Macbeth's face changed. Gone was the flickering doubt, the haunted glances into invisible realms. In its place grew something colder, harder, an armour forged from fatal certainty.

"Time is always one step ahead of me, stealing the chance to act. A fleeting thought means nothing if it isn't matched with action."

He strode across the chamber now, no longer a man hunted by visions, but a hunter.

"From this moment on, the moment I feel something—I'll do it. No more hesitation. Thought and action will come as one."

Lennox did not speak. He stood still, but every muscle seemed taut with a single, unspoken thought: Let him not look at me. Let this fire burn past me.

"And right now—I'll prove my resolve with action. What I decide, I will do." His hand dropped to his sword.

"I'll strike Macduff's castle without warning. I'll take Fife by force. His wife, his children, all unfortunate souls that trace him in his line —I'll kill them all."

There was no rhetoric in his tone, no grandeur — only bleak arithmetic.

"No boasting like a fool," he murmured. "This deed I'll do before this purpose cool."

He stopped suddenly. His gaze darkened, as though remembering the visions that had danced before him.

"But no more sights."

He turned sharply toward Lennox, whose eyes snapped forward in practiced obedience. Macbeth did not seem to notice — or perhaps did not care.

"Where are these gentlemen? Come, bring me where they are."

Lennox bowed, too low, and gestured stiffly toward the outer hall. He did not meet the king's eyes, not as Macbeth swept past him with the momentum of fury.

But as the door creaked shut behind them, Lennox lingered for a heartbeat. His hand brushed the edge of the cold hearth, his face turned toward the empty cauldron. The stones were blackened, cracked. The air no longer stank of magic — only smoke and something charred beneath it.

His eyes narrowed. A flicker passed across his face like the shadow of a raven's wing.

And then he was gone.

ACT IV SCENE 2

The chamber was thick with the hush of unease, like a breath held too long. Lady Macduff stood at the centre of the room as if caught in the stillness between lightning and thunder. The wind moaned faintly beyond the thick stone walls of Fife, and the tapestries stirred, restless, like thoughts that would not still. The fire crackled in the hearth, but its warmth felt distant. Her son sat near her feet, drawing circles in the ash with a stick and humming some childish tune to himself, blissfully unaware that the world had grown fangs.

"What had he done," she asked, not for the first time, "to make him flee the land like a coward in the night?"

Ross shifted uncomfortably by the fire. His cloak was still dusted with frost. "You must have patience, madam."

Lady Macduff turned to him, her face ashen, her gaze sharp. "He had none. No patience. No thought. His flight was madness. When our deeds do not betray us, our fear will — and so we are judged traitors, even if our hearts are clean."

"You do not know," Ross said gently, "whether it was wisdom or fear that drove him."

"Wisdom?" she spat. "To leave me, his babes, his house, his name? To leave them in a place from which he himself has fled like a hare chased down by hounds? You may call that wisdom — I call it cowardice."

She turned away from him and stared into the fire. "He loves us not. A man who loves cannot run while his house burns. Even the wren, the smallest of birds, will fight against the owl if her chicks are threatened in the nest. Fear, yes — he may have felt fear. But there is no love in such fear. Nor wisdom. For what wise man runs headlong against all reason?"

Ross looked at her then, and though the lines of worry crossed his brow, there was affection, too, and sorrow. "My dearest cousin," he said, "I pray you, school your heart. Your husband is no fool — he is noble, and judicious. He knows how these times twist the seasons. I dare not speak more, but I will say this: cruelty reigns. Treason walks in daylight, and we do not know ourselves. We clutch at rumour, call it truth, and fear becomes our compass."

He sighed, deeply. "We drift, all of us, on a sea wild and violent. Each wave strikes a new direction. But I must go. It shall not be long — I will return."

He crouched before the child, brushing a hand lightly over the boy's unruly curls. "Blessing upon you, my pretty cousin."

Lady Macduff's voice was quiet, but it cut the silence like a blade. "Fathered he is… yet he is fatherless."

Ross's eyes stung. "If I stay, I am undone," he whispered. "And so I leave, though my heart is wrenched." And with that, he was gone.

Lady Macduff turned to her son, folding her arms. "Sirrah," she said, forcing a playful air into her tone, "your father's dead."

The boy looked up, blinking. "And what shall I do now? How will I live?"

"As birds do," she said, teasing. "With worms and flies, I suppose."

"With what I get," the boy replied. "That's what birds do."

She laughed softly, and shook her head. "Poor bird. You've no fear of nets, nor lime, nor traps."

"Why should I, mother? Poor birds are not hunted. My father's not dead. Not truly. I don't believe you. If he were "

"He is," she said. "And how wilt thou do for a father?"

He cocked his head. "Nay, how will you do for a husband?"

She raised a brow. "I can buy me twenty at market."

"Then you'll buy them to sell again," the boy grinned, triumphant.

"You speak with all your wit," she said fondly, "and yet it's enough for the both of us."

He paused, thoughtful. "Was my father a traitor?"

"Ay, that he was."

"What is a traitor?"

"One who swears and lies."

"Are all who swear and lie traitors?"

"Every one that does so is a traitor, and must be hanged."

"And must they all be hanged that swear and lie?"

"Every one."v

"Who must hang them?"

"Why, the honest men."

The boy's eyes brightened with mischief. "Then the liars and swearers are fools — for there are more of them than honest men. Why not hang up the honest ones instead?"

Lady Macduff laughed. "God help thee, poor monkey. And how wilt thou do for a father?"

"If he were dead, you would weep," the boy said with perfect logic. "If you do not weep, then I'll know he lives. Or you plan to find me a new one."

"Poor prattler," she whispered, brushing a thumb over his cheek. "How you natter."

And in that moment, the laughter faded from her face.

For footsteps echoed in the hall. And the air grew cold.

The boy had gone to the window to peer through the shutters, his hands smudged with ash, his cheeks flushed with clever defiance. Lady Macduff watched him, love braided with a fear she had not named. Her smile lingered on her lips, but it trembled like the wick of a candle about to drown in its own wax.

The door opened, as though the cold itself had turned the latch. It was not the wind. A man stepped through, wrapped in a traveller's cloak, wet with the breath of the hills. His eyes flicked once about the room, and when they fell on Lady Macduff, they did not linger long.

He looked road-worn, his robes dark with rain, but there was something rigid in his bearing—something soldierly beneath the Church's colours. His boots were caked in the red clay of the south road. From his belt hung both a satchel sealed with a wax mark of Dunkeld, and a short-bladed sword, dulled with use.

"Bless you, fair dame," he said, his voice roughened by haste, but without hostility. "You do not know me, but I know your station. I ride on behalf of the cloister at Dunkeld. Your lord entrusted your safety to the Church."

Lady Macduff took a step forward, protective, poised. "Then speak quickly if you come as friend."

"I do not doubt some danger walks these halls even now." He looked toward the rear of the house, as if something far colder stood beyond the hearth's light. "If you'll take advice from a plain man—do not be found here when it arrives. Flee. Take your little one and go."

Lady Macduff's mouth parted. "What do you mean? Who comes?"

The man's jaw tightened. "Those who would make of your son a message. Who would leave your silence as a warning to your husband." He paused. "There's no time for comfort, nor for disbelief. But there may still be time to run."

"Then help us," she said, suddenly urgent. "If you truly came to protect—"

"That was my charge," he said. "From your husband's own mouth, under oath. There is a way through the orchard, behind the chapel wall, I was told. I'll cover your flight."

She did not move. Her breath stilled.

"Lady Macduff," he said, softer now, "there are no laws left in this house. Only blades. Let the Church be your shield while there's still breath to raise it."

But before she could answer, a shadow passed across the threshold.

There came a figure. No sound announced him. No creak of boot-leather nor jangle of weapon. He was simply there.

Not truly a man, more than a boy, a youth with ageless bearing. Not a man of this house. Not even a man of any house.

She had seen him once before, she was sure of it—or rather, felt she had. Not a face, not a voice—but a presence, as if death had a shape it might wear for a while before discarding it again. Cloaked in dusk, eyes flat as iron coins. The sort of figure a child might name a nightmare, or a bard might liken to a shadow cast by guilt.

He was not alone. Two more men followed him, but they walked a half-step behind and carried none of his silence. They were older, shabbier, without that spider's grace which the pale youth emanated menacingly.

The man from Dunkeld stepped forward to block the hall, drawing his sword with a deliberate motion. His voice was low but firm. "In the name of the Church, I demand you withdraw. This is a house under holy protection."

The pale youth said nothing.

One of the others scoffed. "And who are you to stay our hand?"

"I am no one," the messenger said. "But I am enough to stand between you and a child."

"Then you'll die for it," the scoffer snarled.

The man from Dunkeld did not flinch. "Then may God mark what follows."

Lady Macduff turned, seized her son's hand, and tried to run out of the back, but the way was barred by soldiers whose faces bore grim purpose.

Steel rang once—twice. A cry echoed, sharp and brief. The messenger managed to drive his blade into one man's side before the pale one stepped forward at last and finished it cleanly.

The man from Dunkeld fell without ceremony. He did not cry out. His last sound was a breath — "Go."

Lady Macduff had heard it. She did not look back.

But her son, startled, turned his head just once — and saw the man fall.

The murderers did not hesitate.

The pale one moved slower. Almost regretfully. He passed by the dying messenger with neither glance nor reverence. He had seen death before. He wore it like a scent.

Lady Macduff's breath caught in her throat.

"What are these faces?" she asked, though she already knew they had not come to speak.

But one of the others stepped forward. "Where is your husband?"

She lifted her chin. "I hope in no place so profaned that such as you might find him."

"He is a traitor," the man said flatly.

Time stalled.

"You lie!" the boy shouted, stepping forward with all the fire of his age. "You shag-eared villain!"

The second man — older, sneering — let out a bark of a laugh.

"What, you egg?" he said, amused and irritated in equal measure, as though the very idea of a child offering defiance was offensive to nature itself.

But in the same instant, the boy moved — not to fight, but to flee, darting sideways past the pale figure in the centre of the room.

He almost made it.

The pale youth did not turn, his movements so fast they barely registered. He simply moved his arm in one smooth motion — a flash of silver across the boy's jugular. So clean it made no sound.

The child stumbled.

He reached for his neck, fingers meeting a warmth too sudden, too wild. Blood poured between them, bright and pulsing. He turned back toward his mother, confusion overtaking the pain.

"He has killed me, Mother," the boy gasped, voice already thinning.

Lady Macduff screamed — a scream that tore loose from somewhere ancient, somewhere animal. She dropped to her knees to catch him, but it was the sneering man, the "egg"-caller, who grabbed her, pulling her back, half in panic, half in fear at what they had just unleashed.

She thrashed in his grip, her hands clawing toward her son, but the boy was already slipping to the floor.

His knees hit stone. His body followed, slow, soft, folding like cloth. His small frame twitched once, then stilled. His blood spread out beneath him like a red shroud.

And Seyton — pale, composed, unmoved and uncurious even to his own actions, stood over him, watching the life recede.

He did not smile. He did not flinch. He just watched with ghostly patience until the boy's life had left him. Only when the boy's limbs ceased their tremble did he murmur, barely audible:

"Young fry of treachery."

Lady Macduff had gone silent in the killer's grip. Her sobs came in sharp, breathless jolts, her eyes locked on the body now cooling before the hearth.

Only the hearth remained. Its flame now low.

The room smelled of iron.

And silence returned.

But far in the distance, across the hills and valleys of Scotland, there was a stir—a faint but growing rumble of discontent. The bonds that held the clans in silence were beginning to fray, their whispers gathering strength, their resolve hardening.

And among those whispers, a single name rose above the rest—a name carried on the wind, spoken with quiet determination and an edge of steel.

Macduff.

The shadows along the forest floor seemed to shiver at the name, their edges curling like the coils of a serpent poised to strike. The wind howled through the trees, its voice carrying the promise of storms to come. The stars above flickered faintly, their light winking out as the clouds closed in once more. The burden of a tragedy that would not be forgotten. And in that darkness, the seeds of vengeance took root, their tendrils weaving through the soil, their growth inevitable and unrelenting.

ACT IV SCENE 3

The cloisters of the abbey garden lay hushed beneath a pewter sky, the air motionless but heavy with the breath of coming rain. The earth here did not scream, as Scotland did — it mourned softly, as if veiled in linen. Towering yews flanked the stone walkways, their roots ancient, tangled in secrets and prayers. Beyond the carved arches, a distant bell tolled the hour, solemn as a knell. England's holy court — sanctuary to the wounded, the exiled, and the guiltless alike — stood quiet and austere, its grey stones stained with time and sanctity. But though the walls bore crosses and not swords, though the air was incense-sweet rather than iron-sharp, the men who paced its cloisters carried with them the weight of a blood-soaked land. Duncan's eldest son, Malcolm, was pacing, agitated at the waiting, impatient for action. Years had passed since his father was murdered in his sleep. Suspicions and fears for his safety had forced him to flee to the sanctity of Edward the Confessor's court, but too long had he idled there, getting bitter with the sour wines which were his only comfort.

Macduff joined him with a gait that bore the weight of both haste and sorrow. His cloak was stained by travel and thought, and his breath rose like smoke from a burning house.

"Let us find some desolate hollow," said Malcolm, "where we may unburden our hearts in tears and leave our sorrow at the roots of the earth."

But Macduff shook his head, fire blooming behind his eyes.

"Nay, let us instead grasp the mortal blade, and stand as men should — straddling the grave of our dying nation. Each morning breaks with new cries, with widows howling into the ash, and orphans lifting thin arms to a heaven too bruised to answer. Sorrows multiply like rot in damp timber, and Scotland moans as though the land itself were wounded."

Malcolm turned from him, face grave with something more than pain — suspicion.

"That which I know, I shall mourn. That which I believe, I may yet cure — when time serves and truth proves you. For the tyrant, Macbeth, whose name scalds the tongue, was once held as honourable. You served beside him — you loved him once. He has not harmed you yet. Forgive me — I am young, but even I have learned to read a man's true purpose in his eyes. There are those who feed the wolves with lambs to win their place at the table."

"I am no traitor," Macduff said quietly.

"But Macbeth is," Malcolm returned, sharp as flint. "Even virtue may curdle beneath the crown's burden. Yet I beg your pardon. What you are, I cannot say for certain. Even angels fell, and devils may wear the mask of grace. I would not mistake shadow for light."

Macduff's shoulders slumped as though the breath had been pushed from him.

"Then I have lost all hope."

"Perhaps just in the place where I began to find doubt," said Malcolm. "Why did you leave your wife and child without word? Why abandon the hearth — the very roots of your honour — in such a time of peril? I do not accuse you, but ask only for clarity. My suspicion speaks not of your guilt, but of my need for caution."

Macduff closed his eyes briefly, the image of his wife's hand slipping from his own like smoke.

"Bleed, my country. Bleed without cease. For now you are beneath the yoke of a monster, and no man dares name him false. Let Macbeth wear his wrongs proudly — for they have been ratified by silence and fear. Farewell, my lord. I will not wear the villain's cloak you offer me, not for all the gold stretched from here to the burning coast of Cathay."

Malcolm stepped closer, the edge in his voice softened by respect.

"Be not wroth with me. I do not say I fear you, only that I must be wise. Our land groans beneath the tyrant's boot. I believe there are hands yet willing to rise for her sake. Even now, England arms in our cause. But still, I hesitate. For if I were to claim Macbeth's throne, I fear I might stain it worse than he."

Macduff blinked, his voice low.

"What man could be worse than he?"

"I mean myself," said Malcolm, voice colder now. "There is no sin I do not possess in seed. Should I rule, you would find Macbeth a lamb beside me. I am a vessel overflowing with vice: a devourer of women, a destroyer of nobles. There is no bottom to my lust, no shore to my hunger. Your wives and daughters would fill no portion of my want."

Macduff's mouth parted — in pity or rage, it was not clear.

"Such wild intemperance is ruinous," he said. "But kings have ruled with monstrous appetites before. There are ways to cloak pleasure, to hedge desire. So long as the realm is tended, the people may not feel the burn of your furnace."

Malcolm shook his head.

"You do not understand. My avarice grows deeper. I would rip wealth from the loyal and forge false quarrels to destroy the good. I would hunger for more with every morsel taken."

Macduff's voice cracked.

"This is worse. Such greed has slain better kings. And yet — Scotland is rich. She might endure such theft, if graced with other virtues."

"But I have none," Malcolm whispered. "No justice, no truth, no mercy. I am a thing of ruin, of flame and discord. Were I king, I would pour the milk of peace into the mouth of hell and drown all unity upon the earth."

Macduff looked away. His voice came hoarse, nearly broken.

"O Scotland, my poor, misused home. Must you endure a tyrant bloody and false, only to be devoured by a worse beast still?"

Malcolm stood very still, and then — something shifted in his face.

"And yet... your grief speaks not treason, but love. I take back all I said. These vices I named are not mine, but shadows I cast to test your soul. In truth, I am yet untainted." At this, Malcolm took a theatrical step backwards with his hands raised upwards, though his footing was a little unsure. "Macbeth has sought to snare me by guile, and so I must be slow to trust. But you, Macduff — your anguish proves your honour."

Macduff said nothing, eyes narrowed, mouth tight with conflict.

"Ten thousand men under Siward's banner await my command," Malcolm said. "Let us march for Scotland. For the sake of all that bleeds."

A shadow passed beneath the archway. The man who entered bore neither sword nor sceptre, but his dark robe and smooth manner carried another kind of authority. His face was narrow and solemn, his hands the clean, steady hands of one accustomed to both scribe and scalpel. There was the scent of lavender upon him — faint, yet persistent — and a touch of wax and parchment, as if he lived among both saints and sickness. A healer. Or something close.

"My lords," he said softly. "I bring tidings."

"More of this later," Malcolm said quietly, turning to the figure. "Tell me, comes the king forth, I pray you?"

The man bowed slightly, his voice even.

"Aye, my lord. There waits a company of afflicted souls — wretches grieved by a malady that baffles all art, defies the leech and the surgeon's knife. Yet when His Majesty lays hands upon them..." He paused, as though the thing itself were too holy to name. "They rise from despair. Such grace heaven grants his touch, that they amend where all else has failed."

Malcolm nodded gravely.

"We thank you."

The man offered no more, only bowed and withdrew like a ghost returning to his shrine. The silence he left behind rang louder than his words.

Macduff, frowning, turned.

"What was the disease he named?"

Malcolm folded his hands behind his back, and his gaze turned toward the cloister's far end, where a sparrow flitted among the bare vines.

"They call it The Evil," he said. "Scrofula, in our physicians' tongue. A cruel affliction — glands bloated, ulcerous, the body made monstrous. Yet King Edward — I have seen it with my own eyes — places his hand upon them, and they rise as if from the grave. He binds a coin about their throats, murmurs holy words... and their flesh heals, as though Christ Himself had passed."

He paused, then added with quiet awe,

"And it is said the power shall pass from him to his line — that the blessing is of blood, not moment. Prophecy clings to him like a cloak. He is no mere king, but something anointed."

Before Macduff could speak, footsteps broke the hush.

A figure entered the cloister, his cloak marked by wind and wear. His face bore the strain of travel and harder burdens still — eyes rimmed with grey and a mouth caught in the act of saying what no words wanted to hold. His boots struck the stone like slow heartbeats.

Malcolm turned with narrowed eyes.

"A countryman... though I do not yet know his name."

But Macduff stepped forward with sudden warmth.

"My ever-gentle cousin. Welcome, Ross."

Recognition sparked at last in Malcolm's face.

"I know him now. Sweet God," he murmured, "cut short the days of the cause that keeps us strangers."

Ross bowed his head, voice low.

"Sir. Amen."

Macduff, still leaning forward as if to read the truth in the lines of Ross's face, asked:

"Does Scotland stand where it did?"

Ross hesitated. His tongue moved once, twice, but it was his eyes that answered first — dimmed as though they had seen too much smoke and not enough sky.

"Alas," he said, "poor country. She knows not herself. You cannot call her mother, now — only grave. Smiles belong to fools who know nothing. Groans, shrieks, mad laughter echo like the wind — no ear marks them. Grief has become so common, so expected, that no one asks who has died when the bell tolls."

Macduff drew a breath through clenched teeth.

"The flowers in good men's caps wither before their wearers fall sick," Ross continued, eyes distant. "We die now before we feel ill."

"Your tale is too sharp — and yet too true," Macduff whispered.

"What is the newest grief?" Malcolm asked, though his voice betrayed he feared the answer.

"Grief is born by the hour," Ross said. "New wounds hiss from the mouth before the blade is drawn."

Macduff, trying now to clutch hope to his chest before it slipped away, asked quickly,

"And how fares my wife?"

There was a long pause.

"She was... well," Ross said at last.

"And my children?"

"Well too."

"Macbeth has not harmed them? His vengeance has not reached them?"

Ross looked down. His hands, knotted before him, gripped one another as though one might still the trembling of the other.

"They were well... at peace... when I left them."

A silence bloomed. A terrible, blooming thing.

Macduff's brow furrowed. He stepped forward, eyes narrowing, the calm in his voice beginning to tremble.

"Do not be miserly with your speech. Speak plainly — how goes it?"

Ross drew breath through his nose. The air was cold and dry, as if it too refused to carry what he was about to utter. His mouth opened and shut. A muscle twitched in his jaw. When he spoke, his voice had gone strangely distant, as though part of him stood elsewhere, watching himself deliver the blow.

"When I came to bring the news I carry, the land murmured of revolt — brave men stirring from shadow, whispers thick as smoke. I saw it with my own eyes: the tyrant's forces rousing, spreading like rot across the valleys. Now is the time, Macduff. Were your eyes in Scotland, they would draw soldiers to them. Even our women, grief-wracked and barefoot, would rise with daggers to avenge their own."

Malcolm answered him, voice steeled by cause.

"Then let them take comfort. We come. England grants us good Siward, and ten thousand men beneath his charge. None in Christendom bears more honour."

Ross lowered his gaze.

"Would that I could return your comfort with the same."

His next words came slow, each one dropped like a stone into a well.

"But I bring tidings fit for no man's ear. They ought to be howled into a wasteland, where no soul could catch them and survive."

Macduff's brow knit.

"Is it the nation you mourn for — or a grief more private?"

Ross looked to him — and something behind his eyes broke.

"All of Scotland mourns. But... the heart of it lies with you."

Macduff's throat tightened.

"If the grief is mine, do not hoard it like poison. Let me taste it."

Ross's hands were shaking. He clasped them to still the tremor, but it passed into his breath instead.

"Do not curse my tongue, cousin, for what it now must do. It bears the heaviest sound your ears have ever known."

A silence fell, thick and suffocating. Macduff did not blink. He already knew.

"Your castle was taken by surprise," Ross said, each word drawn like a blade. "Your wife. Your children. Your household — all."

He hesitated.

"Savagely slain. I cannot tell you how — to recount it would be to slay you too."

Macduff did not speak. He only stood there, eyes widening slightly, as though the light itself had turned foreign.

"Merciful heaven," Malcolm whispered.

Macduff's hand rose, slow as mist, and dragged his cap down hard over his eyes.

"Say it again," he rasped. "My children?"

"All," Ross said. "Your wife... your servants. All who drew breath beneath your roof."

"And I—I was not there. My wife too?" His voice broke in two.

"I have said."

Malcolm stepped toward him, uncertain, arms not quite raised.

"Be comforted," he offered. "Let revenge be the salve for your pain. Let it cure what mercy cannot."

But Macduff only stared ahead, hollow now.

"Macbeth... He has no children," he whispered.

The words fell sharp and solitary. Then louder:

"All? Did you say all? O hell-kite — all? My pretty ones? Chickens and their dam? All — at one fell swoop?"

Malcolm swallowed his own grief, then hardened it.

"Face this as a man would."

Macduff turned to him slowly.

"I shall. But I must also feel it as a man. My heart was built to bleed — and it shall."

His voice cracked, but he stood upright still.

"They were precious to me. I cannot forget them. I cannot make sense of the world that took them. Did heaven see, and do nothing? No — it was for me they died. I brought this down. They were struck not for their sins, but for mine. Let them be at peace now... for I never shall be."

Malcolm stepped close, his voice like steel ground on stone.

"Let that sorrow sharpen you. Let it hone your blade. Blunt not the heart — enrage it."

Macduff nodded once. Then again, stronger.

"I could fall to weeping, or shouting, or prayer. But none of it will return them. Gentle heaven — deny me rest until I stand before that butcher. Face to face. Within the length of a sword."

His eyes burned now with something new.

"If he escapes... may heaven forgive him too."

Malcolm's lips twitched — not in a smile, but in grim approval.

"Now you speak like a man of action. Come. Let us go to the king. Our forces wait only our word. Macbeth is ripe for the taking. The powers above lend us their strength. May our cause prove as righteous as our sorrow."

He turned, and Macduff followed. Behind them, the long shadow of the cloister stretched like a mourning veil across the stone. But ahead — ahead there stirred the sound of swords drawn in righteous fury, and the night that had gripped Scotland so long began, faintly, to lift.

The night is long... but it shall not last forever.

ACT V

ACT V SCENE 1

With the weight of late hours the chambers had grown still, though no rest had come to the keep. A wind prowled the stony corridors beyond, shifting in long breaths beneath the castle doors. The walls were thick, yet not thick enough to hold back the chill that had settled over Dunsinane like a curse.

By the hearth, a low fire guttered, reduced to a stubborn red glow. Shadows moved like phantoms across the carved beams overhead. In the hush, two figures kept their vigil.

The first was Maura of Kilbride, silver-haired now but erect in bearing, with hands folded neatly over her apron as though resisting their urge to tremble. Her gown was dark, old-fashioned, the wool worn soft and thin in places by decades of toil. Yet she bore herself like one who had once walked palaces — and indeed, had — before thrones had corrupted the hearts that sat them.

Beside her stood Brother Anselm of Elgin, draped in the layered wool and linen of a cleric-healer. His shoulders were stooped from age, but his gaze was sharp, dark-ringed eyes beneath a thin tonsure and deeply lined brow. A polished wooden cross hung from his neck. He smelled faintly of holy oil and dried lavender.

His voice, when it came, was a whisper weighted with fatigue and doubt.

"This makes the second night," Brother Anselm murmured, turning toward Maura. "And still I see no truth in what you described. How long since you last saw her do these things?"

Maura's reply came not with defiance, but the tired firmness of a woman who had said it all before and been disbelieved.

"Since the King took to the field," she said, "I have seen her rise in the dead of night — not once, but many times. She'll throw her cloak about her shoulders, unlock her cabinet, draw out a folded page, write upon it — as if taking down a confession or command — read it, seal it, and return again to bed as if none of it had happened."

Brother Anselm drew in a breath and crossed himself absently, more gesture than conviction. The candlelight struck his features sharply, hollowing his cheeks.

"A soul in torment," he said. "To be held fast by sleep and yet act as one wide awake — 'tis a violent disturbance of nature. A body that rests while the mind keeps vigil. Such things are whispered of in Rome, but seldom witnessed."

He stepped nearer the hearth, eyes narrowing with priestly caution.

"Besides her wandering — what have you heard her speak? What words pass her lips when she believes herself alone?"

Maura's hands twisted together. Her jaw tightened.

"I cannot say, Father. What she utters in such trances... I dare not repeat. Not without others present to hear. Not without risking my own soul."

"You may entrust it to me," Anselm said gently, but his voice carried the weight of a confessor pressing at a sealed wound. "In matters such as these, the Church must bear witness. It may be nothing — or it may be damnation."

Maura turned her head sharply. Her eyes were full of grief.

"You do not understand, Father. I was there when she was wed the first time, before the crown and the blood. I held her hand when Gille Coemgáin's body was laid on the pyre. Not even then did she show such grief. Not even then did I hear such agony in her breath."

A hush fell between them, more sacred than prayer. And then—

The latch turned.

From the adjoining chamber came the Queen.

She moved like a drifting candle herself — and indeed, in her hand she held one. Its flame trembled but did not waver, casting flickering gold over her pale face and the gauze of her night-robe. Her hair was unbound, spilling down like a veil of shadowed silver, catching at the folds of her garment. Her feet were bare.

Maura caught her breath.

"Look, Father. This is how she comes — just so. She is asleep, I swear it upon my life. Do not speak. Observe her; stand close."

They stood still as statues as Lady Macbeth drifted into the room. Her eyes were wide, but empty — pale moons that reflected light but held no thought. She walked as if down an invisible corridor, her steps deliberate but unseeing.

Anselm stared at the candle in her hand.

"Why does she carry that light?"

"It is never parted from her," Maura whispered. "She keeps it by her always. Says the dark is watching her."

Lady Macbeth paused at the far end of the room, one hand lifting slowly. She began to rub it over the other in small, scrubbing motions — firm and ceaseless.

"She does this often," Maura said quietly. "As if her hands are stained. I've seen her do it for the length of a quarter-hour. And longer still."

Lady Macbeth's voice broke the silence. It was soft — but clear.

"Yet... here's a spot."

Brother Anselm flinched.

"She speaks." He reached for the tablet he had brought. From beneath his mantle he withdrew a compact writing case, wrapped in oilskin and bound with braided gut. He unfastened it with practiced hands, revealing a narrow inkwell stoppered with wax and a folded cloth of dark linen used for blotting. Nestled within the folds was his pen — a goose-feather quill, its shaft fitted into a handle of pale, polished stag bone, worn smooth by long use and marked with faint notches where finger and thumb had rested through many long hours of script.

He took a scrap of vellum and ink to note her words. The quill's tip, honed to an almost surgical point, glistened with a bead of ink black as nightshade. The true power of the church was information, records. Anselm had been instructed to be precise and true, he must report directly to his superiors, his chronicle was meant for eyes far above his own. "I must mark all that she says. I fear she speaks not in riddles, but in truths. I will set down what comes from her, to satisfy my remembrance the more strongly."

Maura said nothing. Her face was stricken with a grief beyond speaking — the grief of seeing one's friend hollowed from within, the soul eaten away by what the mouth can no longer silence.

Lady Macbeth stood in the hush, the candlelight flaring slightly as though her breath disturbed it — yet she made no sound but the scrape of skin upon skin, that same slow ritual of rubbing one palm over the other. Her fingers curled and twitched, caught in the ghost of something no eye could see.

And then, in a voice soft as dream and broken as memory, she began to speak.

"Out… damned spot. Out, I say."

The words clung to the air like smoke. Her tone was not frantic, not theatrical — but intimate, as though she whispered to the blood itself, coaxing it to vanish.

"One… two… then 'tis time to do it. Hell is murky."

She blinked slowly, and Brother Anselm saw her flinch — but not from the light. From something remembered. Her body recoiled with the subtle muscle-memory of a past action.

"Shame, my lord. Fie. A soldier, and yet afraid?"

Her lip curled slightly, as if mocking, but the mockery turned to something almost tender — a tremor of pain in her voice.

"What need we fear who knows it, when none can call our power to account?"

Maura's hand flew to her mouth.

"She's speaking to him," she whispered. "She thinks he stands before her now."

Lady Macbeth's voice dropped.

"Yet… who would have thought the old man to have had so much blood in him?"

The candle in her hand flickered violently as if trying to sputter out — but held. Brother Anselm had begun to scrawl furiously on the vellum, but at these words, his quill stilled. His lips moved in silent prayer.

"Do you mark that?" he murmured to Maura.

Maura did not answer. Her eyes were wide, glistening, fixed on the woman who once held her hands in laughter, who had braided her hair with pearls and whispered secrets to her beneath the orange trees of Scone.

Lady Macbeth stepped further into the room now, her bare feet silent upon the rush-covered stone. She turned her head, slowly, as though listening to voices no one else could hear.

"The Thane of Fife had a wife. Where is she now?"

A silence fell. The memory of Macduff's slaughtered family hung in the air like a confession, though all knew from whom the order was sent. "What, will these hands never be clean?"

Her voice cracked at that. Not raised — never raised — but laced with such restrained despair that it was like hearing glass break beneath silk.

"No more of that, my lord. No more of that. You spoil it all with your starting."

She pressed both palms against her chest now, as though to still a pain there. The candle trembled in her right hand. Her skin was slicked with sweat, her face pale and gleaming, her eyes wide and unseeing.

"Go to, go to," Brother Anselm muttered under his breath. "You have learned what no soul should know."

Maura's voice came quietly beside him.

"She has said what she never ought to have said. Heaven alone knows the rest of what she carries."

Lady Macbeth lifted her hands once more, breathing in sharply.

"Still the smell of blood. It's here. I can't — I can't…"Her voice collapsed inward, cracking with revulsion. "All the perfumes of Arabia would not sweeten this little hand."

Her knees bent slightly, and her shoulders drew in, as though the weight of invisible grief had finally found her spine. Her mouth opened but made only one long, hollow sound:

"Oh… oh… oh…"

Brother Anselm lowered his head. The quill dropped from his fingers and clattered against the stone.

"What a sigh that was," he whispered. "Her heart is sorely laden. I have seen penitent women in plague-cells less afflicted than this."

"I'd not carry such a heart," Maura said, her voice tight with tears. "Not even for the dignity of a queen's crown and body."

Brother Anselm shook his head slowly.

"Well. Well. Well."

"Pray God it is 'well,' Father," she said bitterly.

Anselm stared into the fire, its embers low now, casting more shadow than light.

"This sickness… it lies beyond my art. I have seen sleepwalkers, yes. I've heard confession from souls who wandered in their dreams. And some — some died holy in their beds."

Lady Macbeth turned then, sharply — her back straight, eyes staring into the far wall.

"Wash your hands," she whispered. "Put on your nightgown. Do not look so pale." She seemed to be instructing someone, perhaps herself, perhaps the figure of her husband only she could see. "I tell you once more — Banquo is buried. He cannot rise from the grave."

Brother Anselm's hand had been reaching back from the bone-handled quill, but he stopped before his fingers reached it and covered his mouth, his face betraying his astonishment.

"Even so?" the doctor mumbled, unable to contain the chill that crept up his spine. He had the most awful sense that she was speaking for the last time.

Lady Macbeth turned in a slow half-circle, then took two steps toward the door.

"To bed. To bed. They're knocking at the gate. Come, come, come, come — give me your hand."

And then her voice turned small, so quiet the candle seemed to lean toward it.

"What's done… cannot be undone. To bed. To bed. To bed."

She vanished into the next chamber like a wisp of smoke, the candlelight trailing her like a soul leaving a body.

Silence held for a long moment, broken only by the fire's hiss.

"Will she go now to bed?" Brother Anselm asked, dazed.

"Directly," Maura replied, though her voice carried no certainty.

Brother Anselm crossed himself again, then turned to gather his things with slow, reverent hands.

"There are foul whisperings in this place," he said. "Things done that twist the natural order — and such things have their consequence. A poisoned mind must pour its secrets somewhere, and when no ear listens, the pillow takes them in." He looked toward the doorway where the Queen had disappeared. "She needs more than I can offer. Not leeches, not prayers, nor balm. She needs God Himself. May He forgive us all."

He turned toward Maura, solemn.

"See that she is not left alone. Take away anything she might use against herself. And watch. Always."

He turned to go.

"Good night," he said softly. "She has astonished my mind and unnerved my soul. I dare not say what I think."

Maura inclined her head.

"Good night, good doctor."

He passed into the corridor, his steps fading. The quill remained where it had fallen, tipped into shadow, half-hidden among the rushes — as if forgotten by all but the room itself. And Maura stood alone by the fire, where the smell of wax and sweat still lingered — and where something darker, older, more sorrowful, had begun to take root.

ACT V SCENE 2

The wind howled across the barren moor, carrying with it the chill of the north and the weight of Scotland's despair. The land here was bleak and desolate, its once fertile soil cracked and barren, its trees stripped of leaves and life. Mist clung to the ground like a shroud, curling around the hooves of the advancing force as though reluctant to release them to the coming storm.

Banners snapped in the wind: the red lion of Scotland, the silver cross of Northumbria, and the stag-crest of Moray. Beneath them marched soldiers — lean, mud-footed, drawn from glen and township — and at the head of their column rode four men cloaked in purpose and disquiet.

Menteith, eldest among them, rode with shoulders squared despite the ache in his sword-arm. His greying beard was tied in a Highland twist, and his voice bore the rasp of one who had shouted over too many fires in too many halls.

"There is no loyalty in fear," he muttered. "Those who serve Macbeth do so with knives at their backs and trembling hands. He rules not with reverence, but terror."

Lennox rode a little apart, his gaze fixed on the horizon where the faint glow of dawn was beginning to pierce the gloom. The light was pale and cold, offering no warmth, no solace—only the promise of another day of reckoning. He turned to Angus, riding close beside him, his expression as grim as the landscape around them.

"This land," Lennox said softly, his voice nearly swallowed by the wind. "It feels as though it has turned against us. Every step we take feels heavier, as though the very earth resists our cause."

Angus was younger but sharpened by hardship. He nodded, jaw clenched.

"Scotland suffers, as we all do," he said. "Macbeth has poisoned both soil and soul. But it is not the land that resists us—it is the weight of his shadow."

They paused atop a low rise, letting the army below move in slow formation. The others drew near — Caithness, dark-haired and cold-eyed, his cloak heavy with frost.

"We march against a king," Caithness said, incredulous. "And yet our numbers are fewer than they should be. Too many still cling to fear. Too many believe his crown is blessed."

"Then let us show them he is not invincible," Angus said. "That his shadow can be pierced."

Lennox frowned, his eyes clouded.

"But can it? The man has wrought horrors beyond reason. The witches were seen again — always at the edges of his triumphs. Their prophecies feed his fury. What if they shield him still?"

A silence fell. The mist around them thickened, curling like the breath of the dead. The wind shifted — cold, prophetic.

Caithness broke it.

"Prophecies do not bleed," he said. "He is flesh and bone, mortal as any of us. Whatever the witches whispered, it was Macbeth who acted. And it will be men who end him."

Menteith looked hard at the outline of Dunsinane Hill, when he spoke, his voice now carried more force.

"The English force is close," he said, scanning the far ridge where the sky bent low. "Malcolm rides at its heart. Siward of Northumbria beside him — and Macduff, God keep him."

He cast a glance behind at the long line of soldiers threading the hill.

"They burn with justice — for fathers, wives, and babes. A cause like that stirs even the cold-hearted. It could rouse a corpse from the grave."

Angus' voice was more precise.

"We'll meet them well enough near Birnam Wood. They ride hard from England's side, and that's their path." He looked northward. "But what of Donalbain? Is the younger brother with Malcolm?"

Caithness grunted.

"No one's seen Donalbain since the night their father's blood cried out from Inverness. Fled to Ireland, last we heard. Left his brother to raise the banner alone."

Lennox drew a scroll from his saddle pouch.

"He is not with them. I've a tally of every nobleman in Malcolm's train. Siward's boy is among them — not yet bearded but fierce as a young wolf. There are many such lads in their first bloom of manhood, eager to blood their blades."

Menteith's eyes narrowed as he glanced toward the far-off silhouette of Dunsinane, rising black on the hill like a clenched fist.

"And what of the tyrant?"

Caithness pulled his cloak tight as the wind sliced down the ridge.

"He fortifies Dunsinane — brick and blood both. Some say he's lost his wits entirely. Others, who hate him less, call it brave madness. But he cannot hold the kingdom together with iron and screaming alone."

Angus spat into the mist.

"He feels the weight now — of every murder hidden, every oath broken. The very men in his ranks obey him with hollow eyes. No loyalty binds them — only fear. His crown sits on his head like a stolen helm: too large for the thief who wears it."

"Aye," said Menteith. "It hangs about him like a giant's robe on a dwarfish body."

Lennox nodded grimly.

"Who can blame him for flinching at shadows? Even his own soul must weep to find itself in such company."

The road turned downward toward Birnam. There, beneath the trees, the air held the sharp tang of change.

"Come," said Caithness, urging his horse forward. "Let us give our blades to the one who is truly owed our obedience. Let us meet the remedy that will cleanse this fevered land."

Menteith raised his voice so the men behind could hear.

"And with him, let each of us become a drop in Scotland's purge — every life spent to heal the body of the realm."

Lennox, always more careful with his words, murmured low:

"Or no more than is needed. Just enough to water the sovereign flower… and drown the weeds."

They turned their steeds toward Birnam, where the trees awaited. And behind them, the marching drums picked up a new rhythm — the pulse of war, of reckoning, of restoration.

ACT V SCENE 3

Dunsinane's stones seemed to groan with each gust of wind. The fires sputtered in their sconces, throwing up tall, wavering shadows like the limbs of burning trees. Soldiers passed in near silence through the cold corridors, their armour ill-fitted, their eyes ringed with sleeplessness. The castle, once a seat of revelry and strength, had grown gaunt with doubt.

Macbeth stood at the far end of the hall, pacing before the black hearth. His crown glinted beneath the slivered light, but it sat askew, heavy. The tapestries no longer stirred in the wind — they hung still and soaked from leaks in the walls. He waved away the presence of his attendants, his voice rising like a cry against the void.

"Bring me no more reports," he snapped. "Let them fly — all of them." He turned sharply, his cloak sweeping like a bat's wing. "Until Birnam wood itself comes crawling to Dunsinane, I am beyond fear."

Behind him stood Brother Anselm, still present under orders to observe the Queen's decline — but now wordless, reduced to a shape at the edge of the throne room, a figure of record more than counsel. His cross caught no light.

"What is Malcolm but a boy?" Macbeth spat, his words too loud for the size of the room. "Born of woman, like the rest of them. The spirits have spoken, and I am marked — untouchable."

His voice dropped low, almost reverent "No man born of woman shall harm Macbeth." He repeated it, as though each word laid stone in the crumbling walls around him. "Let them run, those false thanes. Let them bow to the English, kiss their soft Epicurean fingers. I stand unshaken."

He clutched the back of his chair — the same throne from which he had once toasted Duncan, back when the flames had roared and the hall had laughed. His knuckles whitened.

"The mind I sway by, the heart I bear — they do not yield. Not to doubt. Not to fear."

The door creaked open behind him, and a young servant appeared — wide-eyed, soaked from the rain. He wore no armour, just a smudged tunic clinging to his narrow frame.

Macbeth turned, his eyes snapping with fury.

"The devil damn thee black, thou cream-faced loon! What is that look? Why do you gape like a startled goose?"

The boy stammered, trembling.

"There is… ten thousand—"

"Geese?" Macbeth thundered, teeth bared.

"Nay—soldiers, sir."

"Then mark your cheeks and bleed some colour into them, lily-livered boy." Macbeth advanced, eyes dark with contempt. "What soldiers, fool? Your face cries fear before your tongue can speak it. What soldiers, whey-face?"

The servant could barely manage to speak.

"The English, sire."

"Take thy face hence, your face offends me more than your words!" Macbeth growled, dismissing him with a dangerous flick of his hand.

The boy fled, nearly slipping as he passed through the archway, his shadow swallowed by the hallway.

Macbeth turned once more to the fire, though it had burned low.

"Seyton!" he barked into the emptiness. "I am sick at heart."

He waited — no sound.

"When I look upon this house—Seyton, I say! This final push will crown me... or unseat me. I have lived long enough."

His voice softened, briefly.

"My way of life is fallen... I have reached the autumn of my days, and the leaves turn yellow in my name."

He stood very still, as if hearing his own words echoed from some inner canyon.

"That which should accompany old age — honour, love, obedience, friends — I have none. Only curses, mouthed deep. Praise that is breath alone. Words from trembling lips that dare not deny, and do not mean."

He closed his eyes.

"Seyton."

The door opened. He came in silently. Seyton.

He moved without haste, without sound, as though he had been standing behind the door the entire time. He was dressed in a bleached wool tunic. His face was unreadable, as ever. The boy was gone, no longer a youth, Seyton was a man now but still he looked boyish. He had changed little, a blade shaped like a man.

"What is your gracious pleasure?" Seyton asked.

Macbeth's hands twitched as if gripping phantom weapons. He turned sharply, his cloak stirring the stagnant air of the chamber.

"What news more?" he snapped.

Seyton stepped forward, no change in his expression.

"All is confirmed, my lord," he said. "The reports were true."

Macbeth's teeth clenched, but a wild glint lit in his eye.

"Then let them come. I'll fight till my bones are hacked bare and my blood leaves footprints in the snow." He spread his arms, defiant. "Give me my armour."

Seyton did not move.

"'Tis not needed yet." He spoke simply, unafraid and eerily calm as always.

"I'll wear it anyway. Wrap me in iron, Seyton. Let them strike at the metal, not the man."

Seyton gave a slight nod and began to unfasten the clasps at the wall, wordless and fluid.

Macbeth strode toward the outer window slit and peered through the slats. A curl of smoke rose in the distance — no beacon, but a warning. Somewhere in the hills, a rebel fire had been lit.

"Send out more riders," Macbeth growled. "Scour the country. Hang any who speak of fear. String their tongues as pennants from the gates."

His eyes slid to where Brother Anselm still stood — silent, unmoving, half-shadowed by the massive chimney post. The cleric watched not the king but the flicker of the dying fire, as if already composing the final verse of the kingdom's last prayer.

Macbeth addressed him suddenly.

"How fares your patient, doctor?"

Anselm's gaze did not waver.

"She is not so much sick in body, my lord," he said carefully, "as she is… plagued. By thoughts that come thick and fast, and keep her from rest."

Macbeth turned away too quickly, the stiffness in his shoulders betraying his concern.

"Then cure her of that."

He stepped close to Anselm now, voice lowered but hoarse with restrained fury.

"Can you not heal a mind diseased? Pluck sorrow from the memory, cut it out like rot? Scour the mind of its torment — all those crawling thoughts that nest behind the eyes? Give her something — anything — to make her forget."

Anselm's silence hung in the air like incense after a mass.

234

"In that, my lord… the patient must tend to themselves."

Macbeth recoiled, disgusted.

"Throw your medicines to the dogs. I'll have none of them."

Behind him, Seyton was fastening the king's armour, his hands working with quiet efficiency. The plates clinked into place — breast, spaulders, tassets — the old king being locked into his iron skin.

"Come. Give me my staff." He reached for the long haft leaning near the throne, polished smooth by sweat and rage. "Seyton — send out. The thanes flee. Let them. Let the cowardice rot from them like pus."

He turned back to Anselm, voice rising once more.

"If you could cast the water of this cursed land, find its disease and name it — I'd call you saviour, aye, I'd sing your name to every echo in the glens."

He tore off one gauntlet, flinging it down. "What medicine have you? Rhubarb? Camomile? Some purge to scour the English from our hills?"

Anselm hesitated.

"Aye, my lord. Your preparations have made themselves heard. There is word of you."

Macbeth grunted, dismissive, then turned sharply toward the war-room stairs.

"Bring it after me."

He paused on the threshold, one hand resting on his sheathed blade.

"I will not fear death or bane, not till Birnam Wood itself marches to Dunsinane."

He disappeared down the stair.

Anselm remained for a moment, watching the door long after Macbeth had gone.

He crossed himself.

"If I were far from Dunsinane… not all the wealth of Rome would draw me back again."

He turned, his footsteps light, and passed into the chapel shadows beyond.

ACT V SCENE 4

They came to the edge of Birnam Wood under a sky bruised with iron. The branches above were half bare, late in their season, but still clutched handfuls of curling leaves — yellow, rust, the green turned smoke-grey. Beneath them, the forest floor was quiet. Moss grew thick over ancient stones. Birds held their breath.

The army stopped, all motion folding inward like a lung preparing to exhale.

Malcolm rode to the fore and looked upon the treeline with solemn recognition.

"This is the place," he said quietly. "I have not stood here since I was little more than a boy — not since I fled the crown I now reclaim. Then, I feared what walked behind me. Now… I pity what waits ahead."

Menteith, just behind him, gave a small nod.

"We doubt not, cousin, that the days of fear will pass. And safety will return to chambers and cradle alike."

"Not without cost," Malcolm replied.

Siward squinted at the great spread of boughs ahead.

"What wood lies before us?"

"Birnam," Menteith said. "A name cursed and whispered now, thanks to that devil's prophecy."

Malcolm turned in his saddle, his voice rising for all to hear.

"Let every man take up a bough. Cut from the trees and carry them before you — let the tyrant's watchers miscount our numbers, and mistake us for the wood itself."

"It shall be done," the captain of the soldiers replied.

There was a murmur of approval — the soldiers began stepping forward, blades drawn, and soon they hacking branches free from the limbs above.

The rustling that followed was strange — not like men marching, but like the earth itself preparing to move. Leaves fell like murmured prayers. Bark cracked like bone. And in that forest, ancient and vast, it felt for a moment as though the trees had always waited for this.

Siward, his voice always steady, addressed them low.

"We hear nothing new — the tyrant still clings to Dunsinane. He does not retreat. He waits to endure a siege."

"It is his only hope," Malcolm answered. "For all else has abandoned him. Lords great and low have turned from him. And those who remain serve not with hearts, but with hollow eyes and tethered hands."

"I do not fear him," said Macduff.

He stood near the back of the line, having said little until now — his face shadowed beneath his helm, his eyes colder than the steel at his belt.

"I do not fear him, and I do not need disguise," he said, gripping the axe at his side but refusing to cut a branch. "I have no need to be hidden from that man. Let him see me coming."

Malcolm turned, gentle but firm.

"This is not cowardice, cousin. It is strategy. Let prophecy be fulfilled. Let the forest walk."

Macduff nodded once, sharply, and stepped forward at last, pulling a branch down with one swift strike.

"Then let him see his doom dressed in bark and shadow."

Siward drew his sword, testing the balance.

"The hour draws close. When all debts shall be measured."

"And speculation ends," Menteith added.

"From here forward," said Malcolm, "we speak not in hopes, but in actions."

"Aye, hopes make poor armour," said Siward. "What words may weigh, swords will decide. Speculation breeds only shadows," he said quietly. "Let swords settle what thought cannot. We march now to find truth by blade alone."

And the war moved forward, step by step, dressed in the skin of the forest."

The drums began again. Slow. Purposeful. The forest moved.

ACT V SCENE 5

The stone walls of Dunsinane trembled beneath the pressure of distant drums. The banners hung high from the battlements — tattered, defiant, too proud to yield even to the rising wind. Peat smoke curled from the lower hearths where the armourers worked without pause. Outside, the army closed in.

Macbeth stood at the window slit, staring out at the mist-veiled hills beyond. His breath came in sharp exhales, but not from fear — not any longer. There was a strange calm in him now, like a man who has already drowned but still walks the shore.

"Hang out our banners on the outward walls," he barked to the shadows behind him. "Let them come. Let them scream and beat their drums until their hands fall off. This castle laughs at siege. Let them starve in their own silence."

A soldier shifted nervously in the corridor.

"My lord—"

"Had we the men who should be ours, we'd meet them on the plain," Macbeth muttered. "Face to face, beard to beard. Blade to blade. And drive them back into their own dirt."

Seyton had moved to the great doors, pausing at the low sound from somewhere deep in the keep.

Macbeth tilted his head, his voice low now, almost curious.

"What was that?"

Seyton did not look back.

"The cry of women, my lord."

And he was gone. He left swiftly, without a word or a backwards glance.

Macbeth turned slowly, eyes narrowing, shoulders rising and falling with an effort that seemed to cost more than it once had.

"I have almost forgotten the taste of fear," he murmured. "There was a time… when a scream in the night would raise the hair along my neck."

His hand passed across his scalp, touching the place where that fear once lived. Then his hands moved down to the scorpion amulet around his neck. His thumb traced over the amber in which the beast was encased, and it felt almost sticky, as though the resin were still drying after all this time.

"A time when my blood still startled at tales of ghosts, when horror had weight. But I have supped so full with horrors…. direness, familiar to my slaughterous thoughts can no longer rouse me."

The hall felt cold now. The hearth smoked more than it flamed. A candelabra near the throne had guttered, its wax pooling, its flame reduced to a dull orange eye.

Then Seyton returned.

He stood just within the archway. His boots left no sound. His cloak was dry.

"Wherefore was that cry?" Macbeth asked without turning.

A pause. A breath. Then:

"The Queen," Seyton said, his voice flat as winter stone. "… is dead."

He did not bow. Did not avert his eyes. He simply stood, as if carved from the wall.

Macbeth turned slowly. His eyes searched the face of the boy he'd raised — the boy who had stopped being a child the day Banquo's blood struck stone. The boy who had just announced the death of his own mother without so much as a blink or trace of feeling.

"How?"

Seyton did not answer. Not with words. Not aloud.

But in his mind, the moment burned:

A chamber cloaked in hush.

A candle cold in her hand.

The bed half-slept in.

And on the floor beside it, a faint trace of parchment — the edge of vellum curling.

Her fingers had still gripped the bone-handled quill. Though she had not used it to write, save perhaps to write her own fate by opening her veins for ink. The priest had ordered all items of harm be kept away from her, but she had found the sharpest thing in a room meant for silence, dropped by that snooping priest.

There was so much blood, from only two thin, clean lines drawn like a signature across each wrist. Her eyes had not closed.

He had not closed them.

Now, standing before the man who had once loved her, who had twisted her crown with his own hands, he said nothing more, remaining in the familiar silence that had been his confine and his refuge ever since this man stepped through smoke into his life as his new father.

Macbeth blinked once. The news of the death of his Queen a numbness fighting through the veil of his misted sanity. He stared at the fire as though trying to remember what warmth felt like.

"She should have died hereafter…"

The thought came not with sorrow, but as a statement of logistics — there should have been a better time for death. A quieter hour. A lull in the blood. A place in his future where grief could be carved and honoured.

But no. Time had run ragged.

He whispered to no one — to the stones, to the smoke, to whatever shadow lingered in the rafters of the ruined hall.

"There would have been a time for such a word…"

There had been days once, when the word tomorrow meant something. When the next dawn carried with it the promise of deeds yet done, of mercy not spent. But no longer.

Now, time crept.

It oozed. It dragged itself across the earth like a dying man pulling his guts behind him.

"Tomorrow… and tomorrow… and tomorrow," Macbeth murmured.

The syllables tasted like dust.

Time, he thought, was a petty thing. It moved by inches, whispering promises it could not keep. Each day, a ghost of the one before, leading men forward toward the same narrow end — toward a grave.

He could see them now: all the fools who had once stood where he stood. All the kings who thought themselves more than flesh. They too had walked forward, day after day, onto a path lit not by wisdom, but by the burning wreckage of their past selves.

"All our yesterdays," he muttered, "have only lit the way for fools… straight to death."

His voice lowered.

"Out, out, brief candle."

He looked toward the candelabra. One flame remained. It bent low, fighting for breath. Then it vanished, and there was no smoke.

"Life is nothing but a shadow," he said. "A poor player who struts, who frets, who screams across the stage for one meaningless hour — and then is heard no more."

His hand curled into a fist, a numbness.

"It is a tale told by an idiot. Full of sound and fury."

He stared at the wall, where the banners hung limp and blackened.

"Signifying nothing."

The wind shifted.

A door burst open at the far end of the hall. A messenger ran in, half-armoured, breathless. He looked like a boy who had aged too quickly.

Macbeth did not even glance at him.

"You come with words. Say them quickly."

The messenger bowed, faltering.

"My lord... I am not sure I can. I saw it, and yet..."

"Speak, damn you."

The boy swallowed.

"I stood on the ridge... overlooking the wood."

He blinked rapidly.

"I looked toward Birnam, and, methought, the wood began to move."

Macbeth turned, his mouth curled.

"Liar and slave."

"Let me endure your wrath if it be not so," said the boy. "But the grove moves. It comes within three miles now."

For one long second, nothing stirred.

Then Macbeth's voice rose, hoarse with disbelief.

"If you lie, I'll hang you by your own tongue. But if you speak true…"

He trailed off.

Something shifted in his chest. A doubt. A fracture.

"Then the fiend lied. Even his promises were twisted truths. Fear not till Birnam Wood come to Dunsinane… and now the wood comes."

He looked down at his feet. His boots were already dusted with ash. The castle shook again.

"Arm. Arm and out."

He turned toward the war room, robes billowing.

"If this is truth, then there is no running. No waiting. Only the blade."

He reached for his sword.

"I am weary of the sun," he said. "And if this world must end, let it end now."

He struck the bell — the alarum-bell — and it tolled like a funeral knell.

"Blow, wind," Macbeth called. "Come, wrack. At least we'll die with harness on our back."

And he vanished into the roar of preparation, as the forest walked toward his walls.

ACT V SCENE 6

The line of soldiers stood motionless, a forest turned to men. Each held a branch still dripping with sap. They had marched as the wood itself — rustling, silent, immense — and now, they paused upon the rise that overlooked Dunsinane.

The castle loomed, dark against the fading sky, its banners slack with dread. Torches flickered along its ramparts. The shape of it was clear now: a fortress on the edge of collapse, yet still upright — like a madman clinging to the last stone of his ruined keep.

Malcolm raised a hand.

"We're near enough," he said. "Drop the branches."

The men obeyed.

It was like watching a forest shed its skin — the branches fell in one long shush of sound, and beneath them rose the true army of Scotland and England. Helms glinted. Standards rose. Breath steamed in the cold.

"Let us show ourselves for what we are," Malcolm said. "No more hiding."

He turned to Siward, who rode at his side — stoic as ever — and to the younger man beside him: Siward's son, unblooded, but hungry for honour.

"You, my noble uncle, and your valiant son — lead the first assault. You have the right of it."

Siward inclined his head, his hand resting on the hilt of his sword.

Malcolm's voice hardened.

"Macduff and I will follow, as we've planned. Let each of us strike where fate permits."

"Then may fate favour us," Siward said. "If we meet the tyrant's men tonight, and we are bested—" He let the words hang for a breath. "—then let us be unworthy of our swords."

Macduff stepped forward, his armour not polished, but blackened with intent. His face was carved from grief and iron.

"Trumpets," he said. "Let them speak."

And the horns began to blow as a final judgment. Their call split the air, long and harsh, like the cry of warbirds returning to a field already sown with ghosts.

"Give every trumpet breath," Macduff shouted. "Those clamorous harbingers of blood and death."

The soldiers surged forward — not in chaos, but with unity. With order. With purpose.

The leaves lay scattered behind them, like the cast-off lies of a prophecy fulfilled.

ACT V SCENE 7

The clash of steel rang like bells of reckoning across the field. From the shattered gates of Dunsinane, a wave of bodies poured forth — friend and foe indistinguishable beneath soot and blood, their cries swallowed by smoke and wind. The earth itself seemed to groan beneath the press of violence.

And above it all stood Macbeth — blood-streaked, half-armoured, sword drawn, breath sharp in his lungs like a knife edge honed by prophecy.

"They have tied me to a stake," he said aloud, to no one, or to the world itself. "And like a bear, I must fight the course."

His voice was iron through the storm, steady despite the ruin. His limbs ached, but not from age — from memory. The ghost of every death he had caused marched behind his eyes, a slow procession of consequences.

He scanned the field.

"What man is he," he muttered, "who was not born of woman?"

The witches' riddle burned in him still — a threadbare shield, stretched and tattered, but clutched as if belief could make it hold.

He turned toward movement — a figure cutting through the smoke.

Young Siward, Osbeorn, heir to the Earl of Northumbria.

Bare-faced, breath quick, blade drawn. His tabard bore the white crest of Northumbria, already stained with blood. He looked not like a child, but like a man just made — fire in his eyes, steel in his spine.

"What is thy name?" he demanded, voice raised to meet the roar.

Macbeth did not hesitate.

"You'll be afraid to hear it."

"No," the boy shot back. "Even if you call yourself a hotter name than any is in hell, I'll not flinch."

There was something in that — not just defiance, but purpose. Macbeth smiled faintly, as though some half-forgotten part of him admired it.

"My name's Macbeth."

Young Siward's expression twisted.

"The devil himself could not speak a name more hateful to mine ear."

"No, nor more fearful."

"Liar," the boy spat. "Abhorred tyrant. I'll prove it with steel."

He lunged. Their swords met with a shriek of iron — youth against experience, fury against form. Sparks flew. They circled through flame-lit smoke, each blow casting shadows taller than men.

Macbeth parried easily at first — calm, cold, precise. Young Siward pressed, fast and earnest, his strikes hungry. But hunger, Macbeth knew, was not enough.

"You fight well," he said, blade turning the boy's thrust aside. "But you were born of woman. And so —"

His next strike found its mark. The boy staggered, steel parting cloth, then flesh. A sharp breath — and then silence.

Young Siward fell.

Macbeth stood over the body, breathing hard. Not triumphant. Not haunted. Just still.

"Thou wast born of woman," he said again, as if confirming a fact. "And swords I smile at. Weapons I scorn. Brandished by man… of a woman born."

He turned, the sounds of battle swallowing his footsteps. The scorpions in his mind dancing like the witches, tails poised to strike. For if death came for him, it would not come from a boy with a name.

It would come from whatever walked behind the prophecy.

The trumpets screamed again, their pitch higher now — like hawks descending in fury. The battlefield shook with the footfalls of the dying and the victorious alike. Somewhere to the east, a breach had opened in the walls. The tyrant's hold was cracking.

Macduff moved like a man hunting thunder.

Ash dusted his face, and the blood on his sword had dried in patches, dark as iron bark. He moved past fallen soldiers without a glance, eyes fixed ahead — toward the keep, where cries still rang.

"That way," he growled. "That's where the noise is loudest."

The clangour of clashing blades echoed between the stones, and still the one voice he sought had not cried out.

"Show thy face, tyrant. Let it be mine hand that brings you down — else my wife and children will never rest."

He passed a dying soldier whose weapon had never even left its sheath.

"I strike no kerns," he muttered. "Only you, Macbeth. My sword has but one name to answer."

He moved faster now, the sound growing louder, clearer. Somewhere ahead, a figure of power made the ground tremble. Macduff raised his sword to the storm.

"Let me find him, Fortune. And I ask nothing more."

Elsewhere, Malcolm and Siward moved through the broken gates, their standard-bearers trailing close behind.

"This way, my lord," said Siward. "The castle yields easily."

Soldiers passed them — some shouting victory, others silent with blood on their helms.

"Even his own turn blades against him," Siward continued. "The day is yours, my prince. The thanes fight like lions."

"We've found enemies," Malcolm said, "who now strike beside us."

"Then enter. The tyrant's time is through."

And with that, they vanished into the keep, following the sound of trumpets and clashing steel.

Smoke twisted. The wind screamed through shattered stone. And Macbeth emerged once more — his armour dented, blood on his gauntlets not his own, his breath harsh but unshaken.

"Why should I die the Roman fool," he muttered, "and fall on my own sword, while life still runs in others' veins?"

He turned toward the sound behind him.

Macduff.

"Turn, hell-hound," Macduff roared. "Turn!"

Macbeth stopped.

"Of all men, I have avoided you," he said, his voice lower now, wearier. "But go back. My soul is too much charged with your blood already."

"My voice is in my sword: you bloody villain," Macduff snarled. "I have no words, only this."

His blade swung forward. Macbeth blocked it — sparks leapt like fireflies.

"You waste your strength," Macbeth growled. "Your sword may cut the wind as well as me."

Steel rang again, louder this time.

"I bear a charmed life. No man of woman born can kill me."

Macduff's eyes blazed.

"Then despair, Macbeth," he said, stepping in. "For I was from my mother's womb untimely ripped."

Macbeth froze.

254

His hands dropped slightly. His gaze unfocused for a moment — he felt it as a rupture.

"Cursed be that tongue," he whispered, "that speaks my end."

The witches' words spun through his mind, unravelled.

"Those fiends — they lied in truths. Spoke promises like riddles. I was a fool to believe them…"

He raised his sword again, but slower now.

"I'll not fight you."

"Then yield," said Macduff. "Be paraded through the streets. Made into a living lesson. 'Here may you see the tyrant.'"

Macbeth's spine straightened.

"I will not kneel to Malcolm. I will not wear chains. Though the wood came to Dunsinane, and though you are no woman-born, I'll fight to the last."

He raised his blade, the light catching on its edge.

"Before my body I throw my shield. Lay on, Macduff."

He bared his teeth.

"And damned be he that first cries, 'Hold, enough!'"

And they clashed — steel against steel, rage against ruin — as the last light of day vanished behind the smoke.

Macbeth fought like a man unmade — precise, savage, driven not by hope but by defiance. The scorpion amulet at his throat swung wildly with each strike, flashing gold in the half-light. The thing inside it, frozen in its moment of eternal sting, seemed to tremble with each heartbeat.

But Macduff's blade was righteous, and cold.

He pressed forward, blow after blow, pushing the tyrant back across the stones slick with blood. Their swords locked once more — but Macbeth's breath had grown shallow, his arm slower. Fate, and grief, and prophecy had hollowed him. He broke the lock, staggered—

—and Macduff's blade found the opening.

A single stroke. Swift. Final.

The head fell with a sound like thunder muffled in ash.

And Macbeth's body dropped beside it, his limbs folding not like a warrior's, but like a man finally freed from the weight of himself.

A moment later, the scorpion amulet slipped its chain. It struck the stone — a soft, crystalline clink — and rolled.

Amber caught the light. The creature inside lay still.

Coiled. Preserved. Unchanged.

Macduff looked down at the amulet, but did not touch it.

He turned instead to gather the head, the tyrant's face still twisted in that last unyielding snarl — more defiant than afraid.

"Let the curse die with the crown," he murmured. And he walked back through the broken gates.

Behind him, the amulet lay in dust and shadow — as if waiting.

The courtyard still smoked. Spears leaned against the walls like splintered branches. The dead had been cleared, but the ground remembered them — the blood soaked deep into stone, into soil. Torches burned low, their flames no longer signalling war, but mourning.

Malcolm stood among the survivors, his cloak scorched, his circlet still askew from battle.

"Would that all our missing friends had lived to see this day," he said, voice quiet but steady.

Siward nodded, his hands clasped at the small of his back.

"Some must fall," he said. "And yet — for such a day as this — the price is small."

Malcolm turned, brow furrowed.

"Macduff is not yet returned. Nor your son."

At that, Ross stepped forward. He looked exhausted, his mouth dry with dust and bad news.

"Your son, my lord… has paid the soldier's debt."

He bowed his head.

"He lived until he became a man. And once he stood as such — unflinching where he fought — he died as one."

Siward stared at him a long moment.

"Then he is dead?"

"Aye. And brought off the field. But mourn him not by measure of his worth. If you did, you would never cease mourning."

Siward's voice, when it came, was deep and even.

"Were his wounds at his front?"

"Aye. Every one."

Siward exhaled.

"Then let him be God's soldier. I would not trade such a death for a thousand lesser lives."

He stood straighter.

"Had I as many sons as I have hairs, I'd not wish them a fairer end."

He looked upward, toward the fractured sky.

"So let the bell toll. He has earned it."

Malcolm placed a hand upon his shoulder — but before more could be said, a cry rang out from the ruined hall.

Macduff had returned.

And in his grasp, held by the hair, was the severed head of Macbeth — its crown fallen, its eyes half-lidded, its mouth twisted not in rage, but something close to surprise.

Macduff stepped forward, and his voice carried like steel rung clean.

"Hail, king — for so thou art."

He threw the head to the ground, and it struck the stone with a dull, wet thud.

"Behold the usurper. The time is free. The tyrant's breath is ended."

He looked to Malcolm, surrounded by thanes — the noble pearl of Scotland's battered crown.

"These men already hail you in their hearts. Let them speak it aloud."

He turned to them all.

"Hail, King of Scotland."

And as one, they answered:

"Hail, King of Scotland!"

Their voices rose not in joy, but in exhausted reverence. A hymn not of victory, but of survival.

Malcolm stepped forward, his eyes sweeping the courtyard — every man bloodied, every soul changed.

"We shall not spend many words before repaying the debts we owe. You who stood with me — my kinsmen, my thanes — from this day forward, be named Earls, the first in Scotland so honoured."

The nobles bowed.

"There is more to do — we must call home our exiled friends, those who fled the snares of the dead butcher. We must hunt down the cruel hands that served his will."

He hesitated, weighing his words carefully.

"And the queen. Fiend-like, as the world now calls her. She too has died — by her own hand, so it's said. Let the earth close over that."

The torches flickered.

"But for all else… we shall meet the hour with measure, with grace. With time."

He raised his head, and the crown — not of gold, but of oak and steel — was placed upon it.

"Thanks to all, at once and each one. Come — let us go to Scone. And let a new chapter be written."

And as the banners were raised again, no longer torn, and the trumpets sounded not for war, but for a king restored — the wind passed gently through the leaves outside the castle walls.

Essays on Macbeth

As an 80s and 90s child growing up in England, I was lucky enough to go to actual bonfires on Guy Fawkes Night. The smell of gunpowder smoke, burning wood and toffee apples under the cold black November sky filled the small village nestled deep in the Yorkshire Dales. The way the entire village would get excited about building the great pyre on which the unfortunate Guy would be burned. This tradition dates back to November 5th 1605, of course. The real Guy Fawkes, born in York where I went to uni to study literature, was basically a Catholic terrorist who plotted to blow up King James I and the houses of parliament. He's still recognised in popular culture around the world, and (thanks to *V For Vendetta*) his visage is now the logo of the hacktivist group Anonymous. I always felt a bit sorry for Guy Fawkes — his soul must be pretty tired from all the effigies burned annually up and down the nation. Bad enough that he was tortured before being hanged, drawn and quartered in January 1606. Although the earliest documented performance was in 1611 at the Globe Theatre, it's widely accepted Macbeth was written and likely performed in 1606, which *not* incidentally was only a few months after the events of the Gunpowder Plot. Was *Macbeth* basically some kind of propaganda, or an ingratiating homage to the King, written to assuage any doubts about Shakespeare's own theological allegiances?

Shakespeare's *Macbeth* is one of his most iconic tragedies, a dark and gripping exploration of unchecked ambition, guilt, and moral corruption. Central to the play is the titular character, Macbeth, who transforms from a valiant warrior to a tyrannical murderer driven by prophecy and personal ambition. But why did Shakespeare depict him as a villain? Historical records paint a far more nuanced picture of the real Macbeth, a capable ruler whose 17-year reign was relatively stable. The answer lies in a combination of political expediency, dramatic needs, and the propagandistic view of history prevalent in Shakespeare's time, all on the heels of the dramatic Gunpowder Plot.

Historical Context and the Role of Propaganda

Shakespeare wrote Macbeth during the reign of King James I (1603–1625), who was also James VI of Scotland. James's Scottish heritage and his fascination with witchcraft deeply influenced the play. Beyond this, Shakespeare's portrayal of Macbeth as a usurper and Banquo as a noble victim was a deliberate nod to James's supposed lineage. The Stuart monarchy traced its roots to Banquo through Fleance, his son, though this connection is almost certainly fabricated.

At the time, history was often manipulated to legitimize the ruling class. Holinshed's *Chronicles of England, Scotland, and Ireland* (1587), Shakespeare's primary source for *Macbeth*, was itself shaped by the biases of the Tudor and Stuart dynasties. Holinshed portrays Macbeth as an ambitious and tyrannical usurper, though his account retains some sympathy for Macbeth's early rule, and also makes Banquo complicit in the murder. By aligning his depiction with Holinshed's, Shakespeare reinforced James's royal narrative while also avoiding controversy by dramatizing history in a way that flattered the monarchy.

King James I and the Gunpowder Plot

The political climate of England in 1606, when Macbeth was first performed, also shaped the play. Just a year earlier, the Gunpowder Plot of 1605 had shocked the nation. A group of Catholic conspirators, led by Guy Fawkes, had attempted to assassinate King James and destroy the Protestant ruling class by blowing up the Houses of Parliament. This failed act of regicide heightened fears of treason and rebellion, particularly against a divinely appointed monarch.

In this context, *Macbeth* can be read as a cautionary tale. Macbeth's murder of King Duncan—a regicide—leads to chaos, guilt, and Macbeth's ultimate downfall. By dramatizing the dire consequences of such an act, Shakespeare reinforced the contemporary belief in the divine right of kings: the idea that monarchs were appointed by God and rebellion against them was a sin. Additionally, the witches' involvement in Macbeth's rise and fall may have resonated with James's personal interest in witchcraft, which he detailed in his book *Daemonologie* (1597). By associating Macbeth's corruption with supernatural forces, Shakespeare underscored the moral and spiritual dangers of deviating from God's ordained order.

The Real Macbeth: A More Nuanced Legacy

The historical Macbeth, or Mac Bethad mac Findláich, was born around 1005 and ruled Scotland from 1040 to 1057. Unlike Shakespeare's tyrannical depiction, Macbeth was a competent and relatively successful king. He came to power after defeating King Duncan I in battle near Elgin in 1040. Far from being the victimized elder portrayed in the play, the real Duncan was likely a young and ineffective ruler, and Macbeth's rise was a legitimate, military-driven transfer of power rather than an act of treachery.

Before ascending the throne, Macbeth was very likely involved in the killing of Gille Coemgáin, the Mormaer of Moray and his cousin by marriage. The circumstances remain murky, typical of medieval power struggles, but Gille's death in 1032, likely by burning, removed a key rival. It's entirely plausible that King Malcolm II—Duncan's grandfather and then-king of Alba—had a hand in Gille Coemgáin's death. He was notorious for consolidating power and eliminating rivals, often through brutal means. So it's not out of the question that Macbeth may have carried out the deed, but the order could have come from above, possibly from Malcolm himself.

This would make Macbeth less a rogue killer and more a political actor within a violent, dynastic game; something much more nuanced than Shakespeare's "vaulting ambition" version. It also deepens the irony: Macbeth may have been used to clear a rival, only to later be vilified as the usurper when Duncan's line clawed its way back to the throne.

Not long after, Macbeth married Gille's widow, Gruoch, a noblewoman of royal descent. This strategic union strengthened Macbeth's claim to the throne and helped consolidate his power in the north.

Gruoch is better known today as Lady Macbeth, though the real woman was far more politically connected than simply a scheming consort. She was the granddaughter of a former king of Scotland, and her son from her first marriage—Lulach—was adopted by Macbeth. Far from the childless, tragic couple depicted in Shakespeare's play, Macbeth and Gruoch were at the centre of dynastic politics. When Macbeth died in 1057, Lulach briefly succeeded him as king, suggesting that Macbeth had groomed him as an heir and sought to continue a legacy beyond his own reign. In my novel, I decided to attach this mysterious bit of history to the character Seyton, who appears abruptly, says little, and seems almost symbolic. He acts as armiger to Macbeth in Act V Scene 3, and then brings news of Lady Macbeth's death in Scene 5. In my novel, he's the pale assassin and acts like the scorpion sting of

268

Macbeth's paranoid brutality. I had a lot of fun writing that!

Back to Scottish history, once in power, the real Macbeth's reign was marked by stability and prosperity. He is noted for his support of the church and even undertook a pilgrimage to Rome in 1050, an unusual act that suggests his rule was secure enough to leave his kingdom temporarily. However, Macbeth's reign ended when Malcolm Canmore, Duncan's son, sought to reclaim the throne. With the support of English forces, Malcolm defeated Macbeth at the Battle of Lumphanan in 1057. As I previously mentioned, Macbeth's stepson, Lulach, briefly ruled afterward but was also defeated by Malcolm, ushering in a new dynasty.

Modern historians, such as Fiona Watson (Macbeth: A True Story, 2010), have highlighted the contrast between the historical Macbeth and Shakespeare's fictionalized version. Macbeth's villainous portrayal stems largely from later chroniclers, who painted him as a tyrant to legitimize Malcolm's rule and bolster the subsequent royal lineage.

Shakespeare's Sources and Artistic License

Shakespeare's primary source, Holinshed's Chronicles, provides much of the framework for Macbeth. However, Shakespeare made significant alterations to suit his dramatic and political aims. Holinshed's account of Macbeth is less one-dimensional; it acknowledges his initial popularity and competence as king. Yet, it also emphasizes his ambition and eventual downfall, creating the foundation for Shakespeare's tragic arc.

The witches, or "weird sisters," are another element Shakespeare adapted. In Holinshed's Chronicles, they are more like soothsayers, not the sinister, supernatural forces of the play. Shakespeare heightened their malevolence, aligning them with the contemporary fear of witchcraft and using them to symbolize the corrupting influence of prophecy and fate.

Shakespeare also expanded Banquo's role, portraying him as a noble and virtuous foil to Macbeth. In Holinshed's version, Banquo is complicit in Duncan's murder, but Shakespeare sanitized him to flatter King James, who claimed descent from Banquo. This creative choice underscores Shakespeare's willingness to manipulate history to serve his political and dramatic needs.

Dancing Between God and Crown: The Monk at Fife

In adapting *Macbeth* into novel form, I found Act II, Scene 4 particularly captivating. It's a short interlude where Ross meets a nameless "Old Man" in Fife, yet it pulses with unease—eclipses at dawn, animals devouring each other, the world off-kilter. In my version, this quiet figure becomes something more: an emissary of the Church.

Traditionally interpreted as a rustic bystander or folkloric chorus, the Old Man's final words stood out to me:

> *"God's benison go with you, and with those that would make good of bad, and friends of foes."*

That's no shepherd's blessing. It's the language of scripture—measured, double-edged, and politically cautious. I reimagined him as a monk, travelling in humble robes but flanked by armed guards. A witness to regicide. A man who might mourn Duncan, yet still bless the next king. To understand his role, I looked to the world Shakespeare was writing in: post–Gunpowder Plot England. Just a year before *Macbeth*, Catholic conspirators tried to assassinate King James I, who famously commissioned the King James Bible—an ambitious project begun in 1604 and completed in 1611, aiming to unify religious doctrine under a single, authoritative text. Religious tension was at a boiling point. James, a Protestant king with a sacral view of monarchy, saw rebellion as heresy. The Church's endorsement wasn't just spiritual, it was political. And yet, *Macbeth* is eerily silent on religion. No priests condemn the witches. No bishop rebukes Macbeth. The rituals are absent, but the moral weight of sacrilege hangs heavy. That silence gave me space to invent. Into that space I placed my monk. He sees the treachery clearly but, with a glance, calms his guard and rewrites the truth: *God's benison*. A benediction for pragmatism.

This act of rewriting mirrors Shakespeare himself—a man dancing around faith, identity, and authority. Some suggest he was secretly Catholic; others say he simply knew how to survive on a knife-edge. Catholic images echo through his plays, and his ambiguity feels deliberate. My monk is a nod to that ambiguity. Bald at the crown, sharp-eyed, and faintly familiar—he is not Shakespeare, but he bears his likeness. A man who blesses both sinner and state. A man who understands that today's fiction becomes tomorrow's scripture.

Dramatic Needs and Universal Themes

While political factors heavily influenced Macbeth, the play's enduring power lies in its universal themes. Shakespeare's Macbeth is not a one-note villain; he is a deeply human character, torn between ambition and conscience. His soliloquies reveal a man aware of the moral consequences of his actions but unable to resist his darker impulses. This complexity makes Macbeth a compelling tragic hero, allowing audiences to empathize with his struggle even as they condemn his deeds.

Lady Macbeth, too, embodies the destructive potential of unchecked ambition. Her descent into madness parallels Macbeth's own unraveling, illustrating how power and guilt corrupt not only the individual but also those closest to them. By focusing on these internal conflicts, Shakespeare transcends the historical specifics of Macbeth's life, creating a timeless exploration of ambition, morality, and the human condition.

The Unlucky Reputation of Macbeth

In acting circles, Macbeth is considered an unlucky play, earning it the nickname "The Scottish Play." Superstition holds that speaking the play's name inside a theatre can bring bad luck, leading to accidents or mishaps during productions. Instead, actors refer to it obliquely to avoid invoking misfortune.

The origins of this superstition are unclear, but several theories exist. One suggests that the play's dark themes and violent content, combined with the inclusion of witches and their incantations, created an unsettling atmosphere that some attributed to supernatural forces. Another theory posits that early productions of Macbeth were plagued by real accidents and deaths, giving the play its unlucky reputation. For instance, legend has it that in the play's inaugural performance, an actor playing Lady Macbeth died unexpectedly, requiring a last-minute replacement.

The superstition surrounding Macbeth is so pervasive that it has become a staple of theatrical lore. It was even used for comic effect in an episode of Blackadder, where actors refuse to say the play's name and instead jump through hoops to refer to it indirectly. This cultural nod reflects the enduring fascination with the superstition and the play itself.

The Ghost at the Feast and Other Cultural Impacts

The phrase "ghost at the feast" originates from Macbeth, specifically Banquo's ghost appearing at the banquet in Act 3, Scene 4. The ghost is a manifestation of Macbeth's guilt and paranoia, disrupting his attempts to enjoy his ill-gotten power. Over time, the phrase has come to symbolize an unwelcome presence that casts a shadow over an otherwise celebratory occasion.

Beyond this, Macbeth has left a lasting mark on culture. Its themes of ambition, guilt, and the corrupting influence of power have inspired countless adaptations, from operas to films. Notable examples include Orson Welles's 1948 film adaptation and Akira Kurosawa's *Throne of Blood* (1957), which transposes the story to feudal Japan. The character of Lady Macbeth, in particular, has become an archetype of ruthless ambition, her famous line "Out, damned spot!" symbolizing guilt's inescapable grip.

The play has also contributed to the English language, with phrases like "out, out, brief candle" and "double, double, toil and trouble" becoming part of the cultural lexicon. Its exploration of fate and free will continues to resonate, influencing works in literature, psychology, and philosophy.

Why write this in Emily Bronte's style

I was tempted to ask the AI to compose in the style of a great Scottish author such as Rabbie Burns or Sir Walter Scott. If not for copyright issues, I might even have done a version as Irvine Welsh! But Emily is special to me. I was born in Bradford and grew up well within a short radius of the Haworth moors of Wuthering Heights. As this was my first real attempt to convert one of Shakespeare's masterpieces, I needed to be familiar with both the play and the author's style, making it a no-brainer from a personal perspective. However, the AI actually suggested Emily Brontë as the author for Macbeth, due to her rich descriptions of the landscape, and like Yorkshire, Macbeth takes much of its darker elements from its murderous moors. I also liked the idea of a female-style, though Emily Brontë was not afraid to get her hands dirty and she was no stranger to blood and death.

Emily's toughness is legendary. One story that has always stayed with me, which I heard told during a school visit to the Brontë parsonage, involves the time she was bitten by a rabid dog in the village of Haworth. Rather than succumb to panic, Emily dealt with the situation with an almost unearthly calm. She walked home, blood dripping from her arm, and took a red-hot iron to the wound, cauterizing it herself. No doctor was summoned; no help was requested. This self-reliance and stoicism, bordering on ferocity, encapsulates who she was, and that was the story which led me to fall in love with her. Her approach to life was often as stark and uncompromising as the moors she loved. Perhaps this is why her writing carries such a primal and visceral energy—Emily Brontë lived in a way that left her utterly exposed to life's rawness and brutality.

Emily's life was a study in resilience against the backdrop of unrelenting hardship. She was one of six children, two of whom died before reaching adulthood. Her mother died when she was only three. The Brontë family lived under the shadow of death, whether from consumption, malnutrition, or the harsh realities of 19th-century life in industrial Yorkshire. Emily herself experienced profound loss, yet it seemed to propel her toward creative expression rather than paralyze her. The Brontë sisters, in their cramped and cold parsonage, turned their grief and isolation into something remarkable. They wrote obsessively, often on scraps of paper, including sugar packets or the backs of used letters, their imaginations filling the gaps left by the starkness of their real lives.

And though she saw more than her fair share of death, Emily's vision was driven by an inner fire that would not be extinguished. While tending to her father's failing eyesight and grieving her siblings, she composed her greatest work, Wuthering Heights. The novel is a study in extremes—love and hatred, life and death—rooted in the savage beauty of the moors. It's easy to imagine her channelling the same grit and passion into her stories that she demonstrated in her life. For her, literature wasn't a polite distraction; it was a necessity, a way to make sense of an unforgiving world.

This is why, when approaching Macbeth, Emily Brontë felt like the perfect choice. Her own experience of life mirrored the play's savage themes: ambition and ruin, nature and violence, the inescapable weight of death. Her ability to meld human frailty with the brutality of the natural world seemed an ideal lens through which to reinterpret Shakespeare's work. It wasn't simply a stylistic choice—it was about honouring the untamed, enduring spirit of both Macbeth and Emily herself.

271

Conclusion

In reimagining Macbeth through the lens of a different literary voice, I wasn't trying to correct Shakespeare, nor compete with him. I just wanted to walk beside him for a while, to explore what his story might look like if it had taken another path—one where Gruoch had a voice, where Seyton had a past, where monks muttered blessings that could be taken two ways. And maybe, in doing so, to shine a little more light on the real Macbeth too: a man whose legacy was rewritten long before I got to it.

Macbeth is distorted by politics and propaganda, but he's also heartbreakingly human: ambitious, insecure, haunted. That's what drew me to this project in the first place—not just the historical intrigue, but the chance to step into the grey space between fact and fiction, and see what might be found there.

History is never just what happened. It's what gets remembered—and how we choose to retell it. This was my turn.

Thank you for supporting independent publishing

10% of the profits from this book will be donated to ecological and literacy charities. We believe in giving back, encouraging reading, and helping make technology more sustainable for our planet. If you enjoyed this book, check out the rest of the **BARD409** series, where Shakespeare's plays are reimagined in the voices of other great authors. You can sign up for updates, bonus content, and new releases at *www.hungrywolf.net*.

About the Author

Richard S. Pinner is a writer and applied linguist based in Tokyo. His work explores the intersections of language, literature, and technology. His previous books include *Moloch: A Collection of Poems Made with the Interference of Computers* and *Augmented Communication: The Effect of Digital Devices on Face-to-Face Interactions* (Palgrave Macmillan). His debut novel, *The Bad Boys in the Attic*, was written during COVID lockdown and is available from Hungry Wolf Press. When not writing, he teaches, travels, and takes his dog on long walks in the park.

Find him at *www.rspinner.net*.

www.ingramcontent.com/pod-product-compliance
Lightning Source LLC
Chambersburg PA
CBHW061951170626
46813CB00006B/2609